Annie's
Mysteries Unraveled™

A Model Mystery

Elizabeth Penney

Annie's®
AnniesFiction.com

Library of Congress-in-Publication Data
A Model Mystery / by Elizabeth Penney
p. cm.
I. Title

2015905729

AnniesFiction.com
(800) 282-6643
Annie's Mysteries Unraveled™
Series Creators: Janice Tate and Ken Tate
Series Editors: Shari Lohner, Janice Tate, and Ken Tate
Cover Illustrator: Kelley McMorris

10 11 12 13 14 | Printed in China | 9 8 7 6 5 4 3 2 1

One

Early one Monday morning in March, Kate Stevens sat on her patio, drinking coffee, reflecting that she wouldn't be doing this if she were still in Maine where she'd spent most of her life. Right now her friends in Stony Point were dealing with mud and snowbanks and chilly winds. Here in Sage Hills, Texas, the grass was green and leaves were budding on the live oak shading the backyard.

The smartphone resting on the table beside her rang. Alexus Lauren, her book editor. Excitement tingled as Kate picked up. It was usually good news when Alexus called.

"Good morning, Kate. I'm not calling too early, am I?" Her editor's warm voice was traced with good humor. Although tight deadlines and crises often plagued the publishing industry, nothing seemed to faze the unflappable and industrious Alexus.

"No, I'm sitting outside drinking coffee and enjoying the fact that it's warm enough to do so."

"Temps are going up into the 70s today, they say. Spring is really here." Kate heard the shuffling of papers. "Anyway, I'm calling to see if you're ready to start another design book for us."

Kate's heart thudded. Each book meant more income and exposure and another step toward a national reputation as a top crochet designer. "Yes, of course. What do you have in mind?"

"Your book featuring antique lace designs is selling well,

so I was thinking of another vintage-inspired collection." Alexus chuckled. "Of course, some people might be insulted I'm calling the period 'vintage.'" I'm talking about the 1970s. Those fashions are making a comeback of sorts. Some of them, anyway."

"The 1970s." Kate thought about the colorful outfits of the period, remembering photos of the long skirts and bell-bottom jeans her mother had worn. "I think I've seen some crochet clothing from then." She shuddered. "One of my mother's friends had a crochet bikini. I can't imagine ever wearing something like that."

Alexus laughed again. "No bikinis, promise. I'm thinking real clothes. Have you ever heard of the model Bebe Morehouse? She was big in the '70s, almost as famous as Farrah Fawcett."

"I'm not sure. I might recognize her if I saw a picture." Kate tended to focus more on the clothes in fashion magazines than on the models wearing them.

"Believe it or not, Bebe now lives on a farm outside Fort Worth, and she's got a fabulous collection of vintage crochet fashions. She said you could visit and check them out for inspiration. I'll email you her contact information."

"That's wonderful, Alexus." Having actual garments to measure and study would make the design process much easier. "I'll do it." Then she thought of a key question. "When will it be due?"

The editor sighed. "I hate to do this to you, but I'd really like to have the book on the shelves by Christmas so we can maximize sales. That means an early summer deadline. Are you all right with that?"

Trepidation knotted in Kate's stomach. She'd have to work long hours to finish the designs and oversee the photography, especially since she didn't have a single idea yet. She took a deep breath, attempting to channel the stress into productive energy. She could always collapse from exhaustion later, after the book was turned in. "That will be fine. Thanks for the opportunity."

"Thank you. I'm excited to work on another book with you. And with Bebe involved, maybe we'll be able to get some extra press. This will be your biggest seller yet, I just know it."

After she hung up, Kate sat back and picked up her mug. This was probably going to be her last chance to relax for a while, so she might as well enjoy it. Birds hopped along the grass, pecking for worms, and sang in the bushes and trees. She saw daffodils blooming in Frieda Mahl's flower beds. *I should plant some bulbs next fall*, she thought.

"Knock, knock." Kate turned to see Vivi Lawrence, her neighbor and best friend, standing inside the kitchen and peering out through the screen door. Kate had met Vivi right after moving to Sage Hills, and they had quickly bonded over a love of crochet, not to mention their penchant for falling into mysteries. "Vanessa let me in," Vivi explained.

Vanessa was Kate's only daughter. She attended school at nearby Regency College where she was studying journalism and mass communications.

"Grab a coffee and come out," Kate said. "There are morning glory muffins on the counter. And chocolate mix too." Vivi preferred her coffee mixed with hot chocolate, so Kate kept mocha and hot chocolate on hand.

A few minutes later, Vivi came out the door with coffee, fixings, and a plate of muffins and slid into a seat at the table.

"I take it you're heading to work soon," Kate said, noting her friend's pink pencil skirt and matching sweater set, a typical outfit for her job as an event planner for a major Fort Worth hotel, the Hamilton Arms. Her short blond bob was neatly combed, and she wore only a touch of makeup to enhance her pretty face.

"That's right. I have just enough time to visit." Vivi took a sip from her mug. "Ah. I needed this."

The door opened again and Vanessa emerged, her long, dark hair still dripping from the shower. "Oh, good. You brought me a cup."

"When are you heading back to school?" Vivi asked.

Vanessa added sugar and milk to her coffee. "Later this morning. I don't have a class until one." She crinkled her nose in a mischievous grin. "I planned it that way so I could have long weekends. No classes at all on Friday and none on Monday mornings."

"Good idea," Vivi said. "I wish I'd been smart enough to do that when I was in college." She took a big bite of muffin. "Yum. What's in these?"

Kate ticked off the ingredients. "Carrots, pineapple, apple, raisins, and nuts. And all the regular muffin stuff too, like eggs and flour. Actually, Vanessa made them. I just watched." She enjoyed watching her newly grown-up daughter bustle around the kitchen, and she was touched by the pride in her eyes when she served her mother something she'd prepared. She'd even made spaghetti sauce from scratch on Saturday night.

"The original recipe is from Nantucket in the 1970s," Vanessa said. "They're great because they taste even better the next day, unlike most baked goods."

"Speaking of the '70s," Kate said. She went on to tell them of her new assignment. "Alexus says clothes from that era are making a comeback."

"They are, Mom," Vanessa said. "Not all of them, just the cool ones."

"Good thing," Vivi said. "Some of the clothes back then

were hideous. I have an old Polaroid photo of my grandmother wearing a paisley polyester pantsuit. Purple, no less. 'Purple paisley polyester pantsuit,'" Vivi said. "Try saying that three times fast."

"Gruesome." Vanessa shuddered. "What kinds of things are you going to make, Mom?" She selected a muffin and cut it in half. "You could watch some old shows for inspiration."

Kate shrugged. "I'm not sure what I'm doing yet. Alexus said Bebe Morehouse has a collection of crocheted clothes I can look at."

"Bebe Morehouse?" Vivi let out a squeal. "Are you serious? She's a fashion icon."

"You'd know better than I," Kate said. "I wasn't sure who she was."

Vivi frowned, tapping her finger against her lips. "Let me think. I just heard something about her."

"She lives outside Fort Worth," Kate said helpfully.

Vivi snapped her fingers. "That's it. She was in the newspaper. I was surprised to hear that she was here in Texas. I always expect famous people to live in New York or Los Angeles."

"Alexus said she has a farm. Maybe she's a country girl at heart, although that's hard to imagine." Kate smiled at the image of a glamorous woman wearing designer clothes and makeup to pull weeds. The old television comedy *Green Acres* came to mind.

"I'll get my iPad and we can look her up." Vanessa scurried into the house. Within minutes she was back and surfing the Internet, her fingers flying. "Which paper?" she asked Vivi.

"The *Tribune.*"

"Here it is." Vanessa propped the computer tablet so they could all see the headline.

"Locals protest drag strip," it read. Next to the headline was a photograph of a pretty blonde shaking her fist. "Bebe Morehouse, 60, adjoining landowner, says proposed project will destroy quality of life on her rural Magnolia Creek farm."

"Wow. She looks fabulous for her age." Vivi shook her head in amazement. "Promise you'll take me along when you visit."

"She does, and I will. Why don't you read the article to us, Vanessa?" Kate suggested. "The main points, anyway."

Vanessa picked up the tablet and summarized for them. A prominent Fort Worth businessman named Slim Baker was proposing to build a drag strip in the mostly agricultural community. Bebe and other residents who lived nearby were objecting on the grounds that the loud noise and crowds would greatly impact their peace and quiet. The roads weren't adequate either, according to the former model. Vanessa whistled. "Get this. He needs right-of-way across Bebe's land to do the project. Apparently more than one road in is required."

"That makes sense," Vivi said. "If something happens, like an accident or storm damage, you want to be able to get people out. Or emergency vehicles in."

"So his project is doomed then," Kate said. "I'm glad. It sounds horrible." She gestured at the quiet backyard. "Imagine if we had to listen to racing engines all day out here. I'd never get any work done."

"Whoa." Vanessa was still reading the article. "This Slim guy isn't going to go down easy. Listen to this. 'We've committed a great deal of resources to this project to date, and the people of Magnolia Creek need to realize that we're not going to just fold our tents and steal away. We're going to make this project happen, one way or another. The area needs it.'"

"There's a threat if I ever heard one," Vivi said.

"I've seen that kind of thing before in Maine," Kate said. "Big-money developers can put a lot of pressure on a town."

"Bebe Morehouse doesn't look like the type to back down." Vanessa set the tablet down and picked up her coffee. "And speaking of money, I really need to find another job."

Kate was startled. "I thought you were working at the campus bookstore."

"I am. But they cut my hours back. So I'm hoping to find something else to fill in."

"Sometimes we need servers at hotel functions," Vivi said. "You get an hourly wage and tips—quite big ones sometimes. Once you're on the list, you'll get called for jobs, and you can take them or not."

"That sounds perfect. Please put me on the list. You have my cell, right?"

"Yeah, but you'll need to come by and fill out an application." Vivi winked at Vanessa. "Of course, you have connections."

"Will do, and thanks for the inside track." Vanessa picked up her mother's phone and checked the time. "Oops. I'd better go get ready." She stood, sliding her chair back.

"Hang on a second. I have another idea," Kate said. "Give Paige a call. She might need someone to work a few hours at Once Upon a Yarn." Paige Bryant, another good friend, owned a needlecraft shop that was a frequent destination for Kate.

"I'll do that. Thanks, Mom." Carrying her tablet, cup, and plate, Vanessa disappeared into the house.

Kate sighed. "It was so nice having her here for the weekend. I know it's silly, but every time she leaves, I feel a pang of loneliness."

"That's understandable." Vivi's tone was sympathetic.

"Not that I have the experience myself, but Mom says the same thing about me when I leave. And I'm a lot older than Vanessa." The thirty-seven-year-old Vivi was close to her mother, who lived nearby.

"Thanks for the preview of the rest of my life." Kate smiled to show her friend that she was joking. "Actually, I'm blessed to be this close to her. Some of my friends back in Maine have kids in college all the way across the country." In addition to seeking a new start, Kate's choice of Texas was definitely linked to her daughter's choice of college.

"That's the spirit. Look on the bright side." Vivi glanced at her watch. "I'd better get going. I have a meeting at the hotel with a client."

"That's OK." Kate pushed back her chair. "I have a column for *Hook and Needle Artistry* to write. And a book to plan."

"Busy, busy," Vivi said. "But that's the way we like it." She glanced around. "It must be so nice to work here." She laughed. "You've seen my shoe box of an office. I don't even get a window."

"It is nice—" Kate's agreement was interrupted by an earsplitting sound from the street. Without hesitation, they grabbed their cups and dashed inside. Depositing the dishes on the kitchen counter, they ran to the living room.

Vanessa was already at the front picture window. "It looks like they're tearing up the street," she shouted. Even inside, the noise of the jackhammers was deafening.

A rush of anger filled Kate. How on earth was she going to get any work done with all this noise? She opened the door and ran outside, heedless of the fact that she was barefoot. She only vaguely felt the soft grass and gritty driveway as she ran toward the action.

Several men wearing hard hats stood clustered in the

middle of the street watching two more men operating jack-hammers. Two water department trucks were parked nearby. The men all wore nice thick ear protectors, she noticed. Covering her own ears, she positioned herself so the workers could see her. Shrugging her shoulders and frowning, she finally got one to understand she wanted to talk.

As he strode toward her, clipboard under his arm, she retreated to a distance where the noise was almost tolerable. "What's going on?" she shouted.

"We have to replace some pipes," he shouted back.

"How long will it take?"

He shrugged. Looking at his clipboard, he detached a piece of paper and handed it to her. It was a notice of water and sewer repairs to be made in the neighborhood over the next month. It also mentioned that occasional water shutoffs would be necessary.

Kate took the flier and stomped back to the house. Not only would there be constant noise outside her studio, some days she wouldn't have water. It couldn't happen at a worse time.

Two

Kate was still fuming about the noisy roadwork when she arrived at Caddo's Coffee Shop & Gallery on Chisholm Street in Sage Hills. She'd been there before, and it was always busy, a good indication of its popularity. She had noticed the "Free Wi-Fi" sign in the window, but she had not needed it before today. Kate took the sign to mean that working there was welcome. *Driven out of my own home. Who would have believed it?*

After ordering a cup of chai tea, Kate found a quiet table in the back. As she expected, other writers sat at two-top tables, absorbed in their own projects and barely sparing her a glance. She pulled her computer out of its sleeve. *Good thing I have a laptop, or I'd be sunk.*

The deadline for her column was the next day. Although she had a draft, she liked to go over it a couple of times before submitting it. *Hook and Needle Artistry* was a widely read national publication, and since her Brighton & Craig books were mentioned in her short bio, it was a stellar opportunity to promote her work. She felt a tingle of pride. *And soon there will be another book to add to the list!*

She sipped her tea while rereading what she'd already written and then settled into the edits. Occasionally she looked online for reference. The only sounds in the coffee shop were the quiet tapping of keys and the soft classical music piped through the speakers. It was almost as nice as working at home.

Her smartphone rang and she saw it was Adam Vargas,

her agent. The older man, a former magazine writer, had been instrumental in getting her book career off the ground and was a trusted supporter and friend as well. "Hello, Adam," she said, almost whispering so as not to bother others nearby.

"What's the matter, Kate? Laryngitis?" Adam's voice was concerned.

Kate laughed. "No, I'm working at a coffee shop, and I don't want to be rude to others."

"Wanted a change of scene, did you? I do that too, sometimes. Those four walls can close in on you." He chuckled.

"Not exactly." Kate explained the morning's events. "I suppose you're calling about the new book?"

"Yes. It's great news, especially considering the advance." He named a figure almost fifty percent higher than her last book.

"Wow." Kate was stunned. "We hadn't gotten that far. She just wanted to talk about the content and the deadline."

"The money part is my job. And since you're selling well, it was time for an increase."

"Thank you so much." The extra money would definitely give her savings account a boost. Since writing income was sporadic, a nest egg was essential. "So, what did you think of the topic? I'm sure you remember the 1970s," she teased. Adam was almost seventy.

Adam laughed. "I sure do. I wore a leisure suit and had sideburns just like every other guy, believe it or not. And before you ask, yes, I do remember Bebe Morehouse. Her photos were everywhere. Julia looked quite a bit like her, actually. All long hair and legs." Julia was Adam's late wife, and Kate sensed their forty-five-year marriage had been a very happy one.

"If you have any old photos with crocheted clothes, show them to me. I need all the inspiration I can get."

"Will do. I enjoy looking through the old albums now

and then. This will give me a good excuse. Right now I'll let you get back to work. As soon as I get the contract, I'll shoot it over."

"That's great. Thanks again, Adam." While she felt inspired, she checked for the email from her editor with Bebe's number. The efficient Alexus had sent it right after they talked. The phone rang several times, and Kate was preparing herself to leave a message when a woman answered. "Bluebonnet Farm. Bebe speaking." She sounded pleasant, if harried, and Kate quickly gave her the purpose of her call. "Oh, I'd love for you to come. How's this afternoon? I have some free time this week. After that, I'll be hosting a series of yoga retreats, and we'll be very busy." Kate heard the flipping of pages. "Yes, I'll be all booked up. So today would be best."

Once again Kate felt the press of circumstances. Things were happening so fast her head was spinning. She had to go today or she'd never make the deadline. "Today will be fine." They settled on two o'clock. No sooner had she put the phone down than it rang again. This time it was Peter Matthews, the handsome homicide detective she'd been dating. Kate's marriage to Vanessa's father, Harry Stevens, had ended in divorce, something she hadn't wanted. There had been little chance to date, raising a teenage daughter. Not that Kate had been ready for a new relationship. But over the past months, Peter had managed to gradually wear down her reluctance in the nicest possible way.

She felt a smile break out across her face when she answered. "Good morning, detective!" She spoke louder than she meant to, and a nearby customer glanced over in curiosity. She lowered her voice. "What are you up to?"

"Want to grab lunch? I've got some time."

"Sure. I can't go home anyway." She explained her

dilemma, and they agreed to meet at Thai Spoon, a Fort Worth restaurant Peter wanted to try. It was on the side of the city closest to Bebe's farm, so it would work perfectly. As she was packing her tote with the computer, the phone rang again. *Vivi. It's a wonder I finished that column with all these phone calls.*

"You'll never believe what happened," Vivi said. "First my client postponed the meeting until this afternoon, and then they pushed it back until tomorrow."

"Want to go out to Bebe's farm with me after lunch? She can fit me in today, so I might as well get started on this book project."

"I'd love to. Hang on and let me check with my boss." Vivi put her on hold for a minute. "I'm back. I can go! Where do you want to meet?"

"I'm having lunch with Peter at Thai Spoon. Why don't you join us if you can? We can leave from there."

Vivi paused. "Are you sure? I hate to barge in on your date."

Kate laughed. "Don't worry about it. It's just a quick meal."

Kate easily found the restaurant, conveniently located in a strip mall. The space was long and narrow. The walls were red, and the vibrant black and gold decorations had an Asian flare. Peter was seated on a side banquette at a four-top table, the only empty spot in the bustling eatery. Her heart skipped a beat when she spotted the handsome, dark-haired detective. Sharply dressed as always, he wore a charcoal jacket, bright white shirt, and gray pants with his trademark cowboy boots.

His dark blue eyes widened when Kate took the seat next

to him instead of sitting in the chair across. "This is cozy. But I like it." He gave her a kiss on the cheek.

"Vivi is joining us," she said. "I hope you don't mind."

His face fell, but he quickly recovered. "No, of course not."

Kate patted his hand. "We're going to a meeting to research my new book." She waited for her words to sink in.

He registered what she said and gave a little whoop. "New book? That's great. When did you find out?"

"This morning." She filled him in on the news and then they turned to the menu. "What do you recommend? I haven't eaten much Thai food."

"I like the curries the best. They're not like Indian curry; they're made with different spices."

"I take it the chili pepper symbols indicate hotness?" Dishes ranged from one chili pepper to three. "I can't eat anything too spicy."

"Then I recommend the mild panang curry. As for me, the hotter the better."

"The panang sounds good. I see it has lots of veggies." Kate wasn't big on fried or greasy meat dishes.

Vivi hurried into the restaurant, waving as she spotted Kate and Peter. "Thanks for letting me barge in on your lunch." She sat down and settled her purse under the table.

Peter glanced at Kate, raising his eyebrows. "No problem. How are you?"

"Just great." She made a rueful face. "Except for flaky clients." She ordered curry also, and over the delicious meal, she and Kate filled Peter in on Bebe Morehouse and the new book. Peter remembered seeing posters of Bebe from back in the day and was impressed that she might help promote the book.

When they mentioned Bebe's opposition to Slim Baker's

drag racing project, Kate noticed the briefest of frowns slide across his face. "What is it, Peter?"

He ran a hand through his tousled hair. "Well, as you saw in the paper, Slim is a well-known businessman in Fort Worth. Until recently, he owned a chain of convenience stores in, shall we say, the not-so-nice areas of town." He pressed his lips together.

Kate read the rest of the story between the lines. "Something not quite right about them?" she suggested.

He shook his head. "I really can't say more. But Slim might not be the upstanding citizen he portrays himself to be. I would keep my distance if I were you."

Vivi's eyes were puzzled. "We're visiting Bebe to look at her vintage clothes, right? What could possibly happen?"

"To you two?" Peter joked. "I hate to imagine."

The women decided to drive to the farm together in Vivi's cute blue Mini Cooper, which gave Kate a chance to look at the countryside and allowed Vivi to "exercise" her car, something she loved to do. With Vivi's favorite country station cranked high, they left the city behind and headed in the direction of Eagle Mountain Lake, one of the area's prime attractions.

With her window rolled down, Kate took a deep breath of the fragrant spring air, enjoying the feel of the wind on her face. "I really should come out this way more often. I love picnics, swimming, and boating."

"You can rent kayaks at the state park," Vivi said. "We'll have to go sometime. Or you could go with Peter."

Kate let that go by without comment. Instead, she pictured

herself gliding along smooth blue water. A feeling of peace settled over her at the idea. While there were many advantages to living close to the Fort Worth metroplex, it had been an adjustment. Stony Point was decidedly a small town and quite rural, really. She had been used to escaping into nature whenever she wanted. Here she'd have to make an effort, but it would be worth it. Her mind raced back to Vivi's comment. *I wonder if Peter kayaks. Now that would be fun. And romantic.* She pictured them paddling to a deserted island for a picnic.

Next, they drove through Magnolia Creek's quaint brick downtown. "This is a great little town," Vivi said. "I love coming over here for lunch and shopping."

"It reminds me of Stony Point." The eclectic mix of restaurants and retail shops resembled those in the coastal town, although the abundance of cowboy hats and Texas-themed names and items were firm reminders she wasn't in Maine anymore.

"I've lived here all my life. I can't imagine moving halfway across the country. Though it would be an adventure."

"It's been that for sure." Kate thought about all of the mysteries that had found their way to her door in the past year and a half. Sometimes there had been more adventure than she wanted. But there were also new friends and plenty of work, not to mention still being close to Vanessa. Yes, she was doing great in Texas, no one could deny that.

"Check your phone," Vivi said as they left downtown behind and drove out into farmland, open fields stretching out on both sides. "We should be coming to the turn pretty soon."

Kate checked the GPS on her phone, which was tracking their progress. It always gave her a funny feeling to realize how interactive the maps were now. Vivi's car was the little dot moving along the road. "Another mile or so on the right."

"Well, take a look at that." Vivi whistled.

A huge billboard stood in a field full of grazing steers. "Eagles Fly Motor Sports Park. Coming soon."

"I'll bet that's Slim Baker's project," Kate said. "He must be really confident it's going to go through."

"I'll say." Vivi signaled and slowed to make the turn. "And the people who live out here have to look at that ugly sign as a reminder."

The dirt road was narrow and rutted, and Vivi had to slow down to ease over the bumps and potholes. "They'll definitely have to upgrade this road for the park."

"I wish they would anyway." Kate held onto the overhead passenger handle to steady herself. The Mini rumbled over a bridge spanning a creek, and then Vivi slowed even more as the road sharply turned left.

"Vivi. Watch out!" Kate's heart jumped into her throat.

A car was coming at them fast, most of the way over in their lane. Vivi had only seconds to react before the two vehicles would slam head-on. Kate grabbed the handle with both hands and prayed.

Three

With a muffled exclamation, Vivi cut the wheel hard to the right, causing the small car to skim the edge of a deep ditch. Then she jerked them back onto the road as the other car roared past. Kate had barely enough time to see that the car was an orange Volkswagen Beetle with big flower decals on the hood. They'd almost been run down by the Love Bug.

"Whew!" Vivi patted her chest with one hand. "My heart is pounding. I thought she was going to hit us." She slowed the car to a crawl.

"She almost did." Kate hadn't had a chance to see the driver. "So, it was a woman driving? Frankly, I can't imagine a man driving that particular car."

"I'm pretty sure it was a woman. She had short, spiky, dark hair and a horrible grimace on her face."

Kate looked around at the deserted fields. "She probably wasn't expecting anyone to be coming along this road. It doesn't look heavily traveled."

"And I can't wait to get off it. Here's the farm."

On their right, a swinging sign stood beside a driveway bordered by trees; it read, "Bluebonnet Farm and Yoga Retreat." Several sprigs of the famous Texas wildflowers decorated the sign. Vivi turned in, and they slowly crunched their way up the gravel, finally emerging into a large clearing in front of a Victorian-style farmhouse with a wide front porch. A white picket fence enclosed extensive gardens that included arbors, seating nooks, winding paths, and fountains. Behind the house, Kate glimpsed a big red barn and several greenhouses nestled among the trees.

"This is quite a spread," Vivi said as she pulled into a small parking area to the left of the house. It was also fenced and bordered with bright yellow forsythia bushes.

"It is. Much bigger than I pictured it." Kate climbed out of the car, grabbing her tote bag, which contained a notebook and measuring tape as well as her laptop. Today she would jot notes about any vintage clothing that seemed appropriate for her collection.

Vivi grabbed several hotel brochures from the backseat. "I market our services wherever I go." She laughed. "That way my boss doesn't mind when I leave the office once in a while."

As they walked along a flagstone path to the front of the house, Kate noticed artistic clusters of daffodils and tulips bordered by flowering bushes. The contrasting colors were breathtaking.

"I just love azaleas," Vivi said, slowing her pace to look around. "Look at that hot pink over there. Maybe I should plant some."

"I think white azaleas would look perfect outside your house. Hot pink against your blue paint might be a bit much."

Vivi squinted, thinking. "You're probably right."

They reached the porch and climbed the wide, shallow steps. Bebe's love of plants apparently extended to potted varieties. The porch was decorated with hanging planters and standing urns, all overflowing with blooming annuals. A variety of pillar candles stood on stands and several low tables near a seating area of wicker furniture and rocking chairs.

Kate rang the doorbell. No answer. She glanced at the clock framed in wrought iron on the porch wall. Yes, she was on time. A minute early, in fact.

"I hate it when people don't answer right away," Vivi said. "I always worry I have the day or time wrong or they forgot."

"I hope she didn't forget after we drove all the way out here."

"And almost got killed."

Kate rang the bell again and peered through the oval etched glass set into the door. All she could see was a steep staircase rising to the second floor. To her relief, she heard footsteps approaching. The handle rattled, and the door swung open to reveal a tall, stunning woman with waist-length blond hair. Kate knew she was about sixty, but she had very few wrinkles, and her creamy skin was almost flawless. *Good genes and lots of pampering,* Kate thought.

Her large blue eyes opened wide when she saw Kate and Vivi. "May I help you?" Her voice was warm and melodious.

"I'm Kate Stevens. I'm here to speak with Bebe Morehouse about her vintage clothing collection. This is my friend, Vivi Lawrence. She came along for the ride."

The woman snapped her fingers. "That's right." She extended her right hand. "I'm Bebe. We had an appointment, didn't we?" She stepped out onto the porch. "Please forgive me. I just got off the phone with my webmaster, and I'm kind of discombobulated. Someone hacked my website." She grimaced. "They connected it to a rather nasty site."

"Ugh," Vivi said. "That happened at the Hamilton Arms Hotel once. That's where I work. We had to really beef up our Web security."

"That's what I'm doing. Thank goodness Ivan is a whiz with that stuff. I'm barely computer literate." Bebe gestured to the rocking chairs. "Please, have a seat and relax. Do you have time for tea? I've also got homemade lemon pound cake."

Kate was practically floating with all the coffee and tea she had consumed that day, but she agreed just to be polite.

She also liked to establish a rapport with people before diving into business discussions.

Vivi perched on a rocker. "Thanks. I need to relax. We were almost run off the road on our way here."

Bebe paused in the doorway. "Oh no! On the highway?"

Vivi shook her head. "No. On this road. We had just crossed the creek when someone came at us on the wrong side of the road." She demonstrated with gestures. "It was a woman in an orange VW bug."

Alarm flashed across Bebe's face. "That was Phoebe Newland, my assistant. Rather, my ex-assistant. I had to let her go." Her brow furrowed in regret, and Kate sensed that Phoebe must have done something really wrong.

"The way she was driving, she must have been upset to lose her job," Kate said, choosing a chair beside Vivi and placing the tote close at hand.

"Oh, she's a horrible driver under the best conditions. She was angry because I wouldn't hire her back. I've already hired someone else, you see." She waved her hand in the direction of the barn. "Martha is busy settling in as we speak. Well, I'm glad you're all right. I'll be back in a few minutes with the tea."

"I could get used to this." Vivi rocked back and forth vigorously. "In the good old days everyone used to sit in rockers on porches and visit. No one does that now."

"I wonder if Phoebe had anything to do with the hacking," Kate said in a low voice. Bebe had left the storm door open, and she wasn't sure how far her voice would carry. "Disgruntled employee and all."

"I doubt it. I'm sure someone as famous as Bebe attracts a lot of kooks." Vivi touched her own cheek. "Did you see how perfect her skin is? I need to find out her secrets."

Kate laughed. "You don't need any secrets. You're beautiful."

Vivi flapped a dismissive hand and made a scornful noise. "I'm going to keep my ears and eyes open anyway. Pick up some fashion tips."

With a rattle of china, Bebe pushed through the screen door, carrying a tray. She set it on the wicker coffee table and took a seat on the sofa. "This is my own raspberry herbal blend," she said, lifting the teapot and pouring pink tea into three cups. "I hope you like it."

"I'm sure we will," Vivi said, accepting the cup. "Do you grow a lot of herbs and fruit here?"

Bebe handed Kate her cup. "I grow as many varieties as I can. In addition to gardens, I have two greenhouses, one for vegetables and the other for flowers. Plus I have fruit orchards and berries. Of course, I had to find heat-resistant raspberry canes. Otherwise they won't grow here in Texas." She gestured toward items on the tray. "Sugar or honey? The honey is local."

Kate took a sip of the tart tea. "It's perfect without sweet-ener. Very good."

Bebe smiled her thanks and began to cut thin slices of pound cake off a loaf.

"How did you end up here in Magnolia Creek, Texas?" Vivi blurted. "I mean, you had your choice of places to live, right?"

Kate thought she saw a shadow of sadness cross Bebe's eyes. The model gave a little laugh. "Not really. Once you're out of the spotlight, the jet-set lifestyle isn't quite so appealing. I inherited this farm from my favorite great-aunt, who was like a mother to me. I experienced some of my best childhood memories here. So, I decided to put down roots and stay."

"I'm sorry," Vivi said, her cheeks red. "I didn't mean to pry. My mouth runs away from me sometimes."

"Don't worry about it. I could talk about the farm all day. I'm proud to continue its hundred-year heritage. I'm trying to make it self-sustaining, and that's why I'm holding yoga retreats here. People can enjoy the peaceful setting and healthy, local food as they rest and rejuvenate."

"That sounds wonderful," Kate said. In light of the farm's history, she could understand even more why Bebe so adamantly opposed the motor sports park. But rather than bring up a sore subject, she took a bite of lemon pound cake, which had a lemon glaze drizzled across the top that was just sugary enough. "If this cake is a sample of your cooking, your retreats will be a huge success."

"It's fabulous," Vivi agreed. "Take it from me; I'm a baked goods connoisseur."

Bebe's smile was wide and genuine. "Thank you for that. I often feel like I'm operating on a wing and a prayer." She held up crossed fingers. "I've never been in business before."

"Neither have I," Kate said with a laugh. "But it's working out OK so far."

"You're writing a book for Alexus Lauren, right?" Bebe appeared genuinely interested, so Kate filled her in on the new project as well as the books already in print. She pulled a copy of her latest out of the tote, and Bebe leafed through it with flattering noises of admiration.

"I'm really grateful you're letting me look at your clothing collection," Kate said. "I need the inspiration."

"I'm glad to share. It's such fun that the old styles are coming back." Bebe stood with a stretch. "We can go inside now, or if you have time, you can come with me on a little garden tour first." She glanced at the clock on the porch wall. "I've been having problems with one of the fan timers in the greenhouse, and I also need to make sure the sprinkler comes on."

"I'd love to see the gardens," Kate said. She glanced at Vivi, who nodded. "We're in no hurry." Although she itched to begin designing, a few more minutes wouldn't hurt.

"Great. Come this way." Bebe led them down the steps and through the flower gardens in front of the house, mentioning the names of plants as she went. "I've planned everything to bloom in waves," Bebe explained. "So we get color from spring through late fall." Benches and arbors here and there formed seating nooks.

"I'd love to crochet out here," Kate said of a seat under an arbor surrounded by rosebushes. "It must be heavenly when all the roses are in bloom." She touched the velvety petals of an early variety.

"It is. I like to sit and read out here. And I gather the petals to make rose water and rose oil too."

Kate was impressed. Bebe seemed to find a use for everything growing on her property. They were following her toward the vegetable-growing area when Vivi screamed.

"Something nipped my foot!" Vivi pointed at her open-toe sandals.

"Where?" All Kate could see was the camellia hedge on each side of the path.

"Down there." Vivi gestured toward the thicket.

Bebe ducked to peer through the shrubbery, then straightened with a laugh. "Come on out of there, Tansy, and quit attacking our guests." She made a come-on motion with her hand.

Kate didn't know what to expect—a small dog, perhaps—but a little red hen trotted out of the bushes. She and Vivi burst into laughter.

"She's so cute," Vivi said. She shook her finger at the chicken. "Quit thinking my toe is a worm."

"Tansy is one of my free-range hens," Bebe said. "She hates being cooped up, even at night." She started off down the path and the chicken followed. "As you can see, she thinks she's a dog."

The four of them toured the half acre of vegetables and herbs next. This time of year, early vegetables including spinach, lettuce, and peas were up and thriving. "My goal is to produce a good portion of the food I feed my guests. Any excess produce goes to charities."

"That's wonderful." Kate's admiration for Bebe grew even more. The woman was a paragon.

Beyond the vegetable area was the small orchard, where fragrant pink and white blossoms loaded the branches. As they drew closer, Kate noticed swarms of bees enjoying the sweet nectar. Then she noticed something else, something unexpected and disturbing.

In the shade of the fruit trees, a woman lay facedown, her blond hair stained with bright red blood.

Four

Bebe gasped. "That's Martha. Oh no, she's hurt!"

Kate ran across the grass toward Martha, followed by Vivi and Bebe. Had Bebe's new assistant fallen and hit her head? As Kate knelt to search for a pulse, she noticed the injury was dead center in the back of Martha's head. There was a slight chance she had managed to turn herself over after falling down, but Kate had a sinking feeling that someone had deliberately inflicted the injury.

With a sigh of relief, she detected a faint pulse in the woman's slim wrist. "She's alive. Call 911." As Vivi pulled out her phone and began pressing buttons, Kate glanced around the grass for the weapon.

"Did she fall?" Bebe asked. "Hit her head on a rock, maybe?"

"That's what I thought. But there aren't any rocks nearby. The ground is really smooth right here." Kate heard Vivi talking to the dispatcher as she searched in the taller grass near the fruit trees. Back at the edge of the orchard, near a patch of woods, she finally found something. A fist-sized chunk of rock stained with blood rested at the base of a tree as though it had been tossed there.

"Tell them to notify the police too," she called to Vivi. "This was attempted murder."

Bebe sagged to her knees. "Murder? But who would try to kill Martha? I just hired her yesterday."

"Is she local?" Kate asked.

"I don't think so. She just moved here from Houston." Bebe began to wring her hands. "Who could have done such a terrible thing?"

Vivi disconnected the call and joined them. "They'll be here right away." She peered down at Martha, her brow creased with concern. "Is there anything we can do?"

Kate shook her head. "No. We shouldn't move her or touch the wound, even to try to stop the bleeding. She could have a skull fracture." At their surprised looks, she said, "I studied a lot of first-aid manuals after my daughter cut her chin at age four and had to go to the emergency room."

"I'm glad you did." Vivi paced back and forth. "I hope they get here soon."

"Me too." Kate leaned over and checked Martha to make sure she was still breathing. She knew the rudiments of CPR, but she hated the thought of someone's life depending on her skill, or lack thereof.

At long last they heard sirens. Bebe rose to her feet. "I'll go meet the ambulance. They can get back here if they go around by the barn." She ran off through the garden.

While they waited for the medics, Kate and Vivi stood vigil.

"Bebe said Martha just moved here," Kate said. "So who in Magnolia Creek would want to hurt her?"

Vivi wrapped her arms around herself, shivering despite the balmy afternoon air. "Maybe it was one of those random things. Whoever it was could have attacked us instead." She peered around fearfully as if expecting another rock to come sailing through the air.

"I suppose so, if there's a madman prowling around out here, miles from nowhere. But I think—" She was interrupted by the arrival of the ambulance, which bumped over the grass into the orchard and stopped near the victim.

"That was quick," Vivi said.

"I'm glad. It may save Martha's life." The woman hadn't moved, and Kate prayed that she would recover. She knew head wounds were tricky.

Two EMTs piled out and pulled gear from the vehicle. A sheriff's cruiser and an unmarked sedan arrived next in the orchard, along with Bebe, who returned from directing them through the property.

To Kate's surprise, Peter Matthews climbed out of the unmarked car. He appeared equally surprised to see her and Vivi. After he conferred with the deputy and the EMTs, he strode over to where the three women stood.

"Peter. I didn't expect to see you here," Kate said.

He shifted from foot to foot. "I happened to be in the area. The county sometimes calls us whenever they think they have something too big for them to handle. 'Resource sharing,' they call it. I was already in the area on a separate case when I heard this assault come in. The county boys asked if I wanted to come with them. I heard the location was Bluebonnet Farm, but I didn't connect it with where you were headed today."

"Bebe Morehouse," Bebe said, extending a hand to Peter. She glanced back and forth between Kate and Peter, a questioning look in her eyes. "How do you two know each other?"

Judging by the burning warmth of her face, Kate knew her flush matched the one on Peter's cheeks. "Well ... you see ...," he stammered.

"They're dating," Vivi chimed in. "But don't worry, they don't let their relationship interfere with investigations."

Bebe's brows rose. "'They'? Do you investigate too, Kate?"

"I sometimes find myself in the middle of a mystery," Kate muttered defensively. "I don't know why. It just happens. I don't go looking for them."

"She's got a great solve rate," the helpful Vivi said. "We'll help you find out who hurt Martha."

"That's wonderful," Bebe said. "I feel absolutely terrible about this happening to her, especially on my land, while she was working for me."

Pulling out his notepad, Peter fixed his eyes on Bebe. "I take it you're the property owner, Ms. Morehouse?" His cheeks flushed faintly again and Kate hid a smile, guessing he was a little starstruck to be speaking to a world-famous supermodel.

"Yes. The, uh, victim is Martha Brown, my new assistant. I can't think why—" She broke off, fighting tears as she stared off into the distance.

Giving her a moment, Peter glanced back at the EMTs, who had loaded Martha onto a gurney and now were transporting her to the ambulance under the deputy's watchful gaze. "How long has she worked for you, Ms. Morehouse?" Peter's tone was gentle.

Bebe shook her head. "I just hired her yesterday. Today she was moving in." She pointed to the barn. "I've converted the barn into living quarters. I can't imagine who would try to hurt Martha. She doesn't know anyone around here."

Peter's eyes met Kate's, and she knew he shared her disbelief that someone had randomly attacked a newcomer. The question was, had trouble followed Martha here or was the answer tied to the farm?

"I'll have to take a look at her things," he said. "Who found her?"

Kate explained the sequence of events as Peter took careful notes. As usual, Kate was impressed with his keen intelligence and cool head. He was someone she was proud to date.

"After they take Ms. Brown to the hospital, I'll have you show me the rock, Kate."

Distracted by the sound of the ambulance doors shutting, Bebe glanced in that direction. "Excuse me. I've got to find out where they're taking her." Waving her hand and shouting for them to wait, she trotted off.

"I have a theory about who might have done it," Kate said quickly. She hadn't wanted to discuss her suspicions in front of Bebe prematurely. "Phoebe Newland, the assistant Martha just replaced. She was out here today."

"How do you know that?" Peter asked.

Vivi grimaced. "Because she almost killed us." She related the saga of how the young woman had driven toward them on the wrong side of the road.

"Bebe told us Phoebe was here begging for her old job." Kate took up the tale. "Apparently she was steamed when Bebe told her the position was already filled."

"So you think she might have attacked the new assistant?"

Kate shrugged. "You never know. Maybe the doctor can tell how long Martha was lying out here by looking at the wound. We'd been at the farm about an hour when we found her. Right, Vivi?"

Vivi checked the time on her phone. "Yes. We had tea and then took a garden tour."

"I know it's premature to blatantly accuse her," Kate said. "Can you find out more without doing that?"

"Of course." He winked. "I'm known for my tact and discretion. I'll ask Ms. Morehouse who else was out here today and see what I can learn about Phoebe's movements." He jotted a note. "Plus, she's a possible witness and might have seen something."

The deputy sauntered up. "What do you need me to do now, detective?"

"Do you have a camera in your cruiser?" At his nod, Peter

pointed to the grass where Martha had lain. "I want you to treat this like a crime scene. Take photos of the entire area and do a thorough ground search for evidence." He turned to Kate. "Let's go take a look at that rock."

By the time Peter and the deputy finished with the photographs and packaged up the rock as evidence, additional officers had arrived. Peter dispatched them to search the property perimeter, which was bordered by fencing. He and the deputy were going to search Martha's room for information. Bebe, who had returned after seeing the ambulance leave, handed him the master key so he could get into the barn and Martha's room.

"Are you finished with us?" Kate asked Peter.

"Why don't you hang around a little longer if you can? I might have some additional questions."

"Is that all right with you, Vivi? I'm not driving," she explained to Peter.

Vivi shrugged. "I don't have any plans, so sure."

"We'll be up at the house," Bebe said. "I'll make coffee for your men." As they walked back through the gardens, she said, "You didn't even get a chance to look at the clothes yet, Kate. I'm guessing you don't feel like it now."

Bebe was right; the upsetting event had quashed her desire to work. Crochet design seemed rather trivial compared with a woman fighting for her life. "I don't think I could concentrate," Kate admitted.

"You can come back tomorrow or the next day, if that works for you." Bebe patted her shoulder. "We'll get you back on track." She took the lead when the path narrowed but then stopped suddenly, causing Vivi and Kate to bump into each other. "Perfect. Just what I need right now."

A gold Lexus was creeping up the driveway, as if the driver didn't want to risk a rock damaging the glossy finish.

"Who is it?" Kate asked.

Bebe gave a very unrefined snort and strode forward again. "My ex-husband and his new wife. My only consolation is that they're perfect for each other."

With that description, Kate wasn't sure what to expect. She and Vivi seated themselves in rockers while Bebe stood guard by the steps, arms folded across her chest. The couple took their sweet time getting out of the car. When they finally emerged, Kate was stunned by the new wife's resemblance to Bebe.

Tall, check. Blond, check. Gorgeous, check. Although wife number two was rail-thin and elegant, dressed in a couture wrap dress and high heels, and Bebe was a bit fuller-figured and casual in well-cut jeans and a light sweater, the women could have been sisters.

"I know what you're thinking," Bebe said wryly. "Derek definitely has a type. I guess you could say he upgraded to a newer—or younger—model."

The fortunate Derek was a good-looking man in his mid-sixties, sporting a full head of salt-and-pepper hair. He wore an expensive tweed jacket and gray pants.

"Hello, m' love!" he called out, holding his wife's arm as she picked her way across the gravel. His grin was wide and infectious.

"He's English," Vivi whispered. "I love the accent."

Bebe softened her stance slightly, a small smile playing around her lips. "How are you two?"

"I have great news." Derek stood back to allow his wife to enter the garden path first. On more solid ground, her gait was pure runway model, all flashing legs and limber hips.

"You're going to give me a payment on that loan?" Bebe's tone was ironic.

Derek ducked his head, the grin sliding off his face. "Not yet." The grin was back. "But I will shortly, I promise."

"That's what you always say. Have a seat, Ariel." Bebe ushered wife number two to a seat next to Vivi.

As an ex-wife herself, Kate watched this interaction with interest. So, Derek still owed Bebe money and was putting off paying her. She didn't seem angry, though. Her attitude was indulgent and almost forgiving.

Derek climbed the steps, reaching the top with a sigh. Once he recovered, he asked, "And who are these lovely ladies?" His bright gaze focused on Kate and Vivi.

Bebe made the introductions, then excused herself to put on a pot of coffee. Derek watched her enter the house. "She's still got it," he said, raising a brow in appreciation. "One of the best I ever worked with."

Kate glanced at Ariel to see her reaction to her husband's admiration of his ex, but she merely pulled a gold compact out of her expensive leather handbag and powdered her pert nose.

"I assure you, my interest is purely professional." Amusement danced in the Englishman's eyes. "I'm a photographer, you see, and my photos of Bebe launched both our careers."

Vivi snapped her fingers. "That's right. I've seen your name in fashion magazines. Are you still doing that?"

He brushed at his tweed sleeves, giving Kate the impression he was ruffled by this question and Vivi's unintended implication that his career was passé. "But of course." He nodded at Ariel. "She was my latest protégé. You've probably seen her in the international Julie cosmetic campaign. And I'm working on finding new talent. We're opening a modeling agency here in Fort Worth."

"That's exciting," Vivi said. "I know there's a lot of advertising work here. We use models for the Hamilton Arms Hotel print and television ads." She paused before adding, "I work there in events."

His gaze went from Vivi to Kate and back. "Perhaps you two would be interested in auditioning. There's quite a lot of work for lovely women over thirty, believe it or not."

Before Kate or Vivi could respond to this surprising offer, Bebe appeared in the doorway. "Does anyone want coffee? I'll bring out a tray, then make another pot for the deputies."

Frowning, Derek glanced around as though searching for the officers. "Deputies? Are you serving me papers?"

Bebe's laughter pealed out. "It's not always about you, Derek. First, I didn't even know you were coming, or I might have considered it. Second, didn't you notice the cruisers parked near the barn? My assistant was ... injured today, and they're here investigating."

Ariel's face was aghast as she clicked the compact shut and stowed it in the bag. "What kind of injury brings in the police?" Her voice was low-pitched and slightly husky, with a definite trace of Texas twang.

Bebe's face sagged. For a moment she looked every year of her chronological age. "A serious one. She was attacked in the orchard."

"My heavens. I hope she's all right." Ariel put one hand to her chest.

"Me too," Bebe said. "I'm going to visit her at the hospital once the police leave." She stared out into the garden for a moment and then shook herself. "Anyway, who wants coffee?"

At the chorus of yeses, Vivi stood. "I'll come help." She smiled. "Maybe there's more of that lemon cake on offer." She struck a pose. "Although if I'm going to be modeling ..." Her smile was pure mischief.

"There's plenty left," Bebe said, entering the house, Vivi

on her heels. "And I've got molasses cookies as well."

Kate told the other two the bare-bones story of what had happened to Martha, with Derek and Ariel interjecting horror, alarm, and concern as appropriate.

"I hope they find whoever did it," Derek said. "It makes me worry about Bebe, living out here all alone."

Instead of making a snide comment about his concern for his former mate as Kate half expected, Ariel said, "I agree. Perhaps she should hire a live-in groundskeeper. She needs one anyway, with all this property to take care of." Her eyes flashed. "She probably can't afford it since *certain people* owe her money."

Flushing, Derek bent down and brushed imaginary dust off his gleaming leather loafers, the type trimmed with tassels. Kate was also uncomfortable in the tense atmosphere that had descended. Personally, she'd had enough marital discord to last her a lifetime. Her ex, Harry, was a difficult man. Communicating with him was like tiptoeing through a field of land mines. She never knew when something would blow up in her face.

Fortunately, Vivi appeared with the tray just then, followed by Bebe, who carried a plate of baked goods. "I've had the best idea," Bebe said, seemingly oblivious to the uneasy silence. "Why don't you act as Kate's fit model for her crochet collection, Ariel? Kate is using my vintage clothing as inspiration for a book."

Derek's head jerked up. "Do you need a photographer?"

Kate's pulse sped up. Having a well-known model and photographer assist with the book would be an additional boost to publicity. "We do use models and photographers, but I'll have to speak to my editor about the budget. You two are much more prominent than who we usually get."

He flapped a hand. "I'm sure we can work something out."

Either he was truly altruistic or really hurting for money, Kate mused as she sipped a mug of coffee. Either way, Alexus would probably be thrilled.

"I'll do it," Ariel said. She glanced at her dainty wristwatch. "But I don't have time to get measured today. How's tomorrow morning?"

Kate glanced at Bebe, who nodded. So they arranged a time to meet the next morning. After Bebe and Derek conferred privately for a few moments, the couple took their leave. Next, Peter came to the house to release Kate and Vivi and ask Bebe a few more questions.

"Well, that kind of excitement isn't exactly what I had in mind today," Kate said as they drove away. "Poor Martha. I'm really worried about her." Peter had checked in at the hospital earlier and reported that there wasn't any change in Martha's condition so far, but the doctors were hopeful.

"Why don't we visit her tomorrow?" Vivi suggested. "The hospital is near the hotel, so we can go over during my lunch."

"Good idea. I'll call you when I'm finished at the farm."

The trip back to Fort Worth passed without incident. Vivi pulled up beside Kate's van in the parking lot and she gathered her things. It felt like she'd been away from home for days, not hours. She hoped the workers would be gone by now.

Vivi checked her phone and grimaced. "My boss just called a late meeting. I probably won't be home until almost seven."

"Why don't you come over and have supper with me?" Kate offered. "I'll make spaghetti with the rest of Vanessa's sauce. I can wait to eat until you get finished." She smiled. "All that pound cake will keep me going."

"That sounds perfect," Vivi said. "I've got a loaf of garlic bread to contribute. See you then."

As Kate turned onto her street, she was relieved to see the workers were gone. The only evidence of their existence was a huge hole with orange cones around it. As she pulled into the driveway, her phone rang. *Peter.*

"Hi, Peter. Is there news about Martha?" Heart pounding, she waited for his answer, praying that the woman hadn't died.

"There is. First, the good news. She regained consciousness, and the doctor said she'll make a full recovery."

Relief swept over Kate. "Thank goodness." Then the full meaning of his words sank in. "What's the bad news?"

"Martha Brown doesn't exist. The woman in that hospital bed is living under an alias."

Five

"Do you think the assault is linked to her real identity?" Still holding the phone to her ear, Kate grabbed her tote and climbed out of the van.

"It's certainly a possibility." Peter sighed. "When working a case, you like to narrow things down, not complicate them. And right now, it's complicated."

Kate unlocked the front door and entered her blissfully quiet house, warmed by the late-afternoon sun. "Just out of curiosity, how did you find out?" She dropped the tote in the living room and went to the kitchen for a glass of water.

"Her driver's license was fake. Oh, it's a good fake. Your average person wouldn't notice. But when the guys at the station ran it, it came back invalid."

Kate thought of kind, trusting Bebe Morehouse, who had hired a woman under a false identity to live on her property. "Poor Bebe. How'd she take it?" She selected a glass from the cupboard and filled it from the filtered water container.

Peter sighed. "She's still on Martha's side. Says she's a really wonderful woman. I hope she's right and Martha isn't a criminal on the lam."

Kate laughed. "On the lam? I didn't think policemen actually talked like that." Leaning against the counter, she took a sip of water.

"Sometimes we do, wise guy," Peter said in a Humphrey Bogart accent. "So, are we still on for dinner at Paige's this week?" Paige's husband, Patrick, and Peter were becoming friends, and Kate enjoyed it when the foursome got together.

"As far as I know. I'll call you if anything changes. And please, keep me posted on Martha. After being the one to find her, I guess I feel a connection."

"I'll do that. Well, I'd better get back to work." Once again he put on the Bogart accent. "Have a nice night, sweetheart. I'll be seeing ya."

Kate laughed as they disconnected. The better she knew Peter, the more she liked him. He was full of humor and unexpected quirks. A great guy to have in her corner, for sure.

The sounds of birds chirping outside her window woke Kate early the next morning. Excitement coiled in her stomach when she remembered her appointment with Ariel at the farm. The involvement of high-profile fashion industry insiders would only help her work reach a wider audience. She breathed a quick prayer of thanks for the grace and favor her work was receiving.

After a good stretch, she rolled out of bed and padded to the kitchen in her pajamas. Sunlight streamed through the windows, further boosting her spirits. As she made coffee, she felt deeply content. Leaving everything she'd known and starting over in a new place had been a huge risk, and for most of her life, she had been risk-averse. Having her efforts succeed was a sweet blessing.

While drinking coffee, she did a little research online concerning the resurgence of '70s fashion. She found vintage-inspired dresses, skirts, tops, and accessories and noted the features that were popular with women and girls today. She'd look at the collection with an eye to what was popular now and leave some of the more far-out styles to history. For fun, she searched for television shows from the era and added them to her viewing queue. They might help her get in the mood even more.

An earsplitting noise rose out on the street at the same time someone banged on her door. She peeked outside and saw the workman she had spoken to the day before.

Conscious of her nightwear, she threw on a long coat before she opened the door. "Yes? What is it?" She practically had to yell.

"Our equipment will be parked in front of your driveway today. You'd better move your car." He pointed at a huge backhoe being unloaded from a trailer.

Great. Now they were trapping her inside her house. "Give me fifteen minutes, and I'll be gone for the day." She showered and dressed in record time, then grabbed her tote and jumped into her van. Thank goodness she had somewhere to go. The whole situation was infuriating.

Ariel was already at the farm when she arrived, seated on the porch and chatting with Bebe. She wore slacks and a silk boatneck top in pale blue with pretty but practical matching slide mules on her feet. Bebe, in jeans again, held up a carafe. "Good morning, Kate. Coffee?"

"Sure." Kate set down her tote and sat in a rocker, feeling herself relax as the ambiance of the farm sank in. This early in the day the gardens were lovely, the sun sparkling on the dew cupped in blossoms and leaves. Songbirds flitted around, darting to the feeders set up near the house. She sighed deeply.

"Nice, isn't it?" Ariel said. "I love it out here. It's so peaceful."

Again, Kate was impressed by how well the two women got along. If Harry got remarried, would she be able to coexist with the new wife? She hoped so for Vanessa's sake.

"That's my goal, to create an oasis of peace and tranquility in our all-too-busy world." Bebe's voice was fervent. "I remember what it was like to depend on sleeping pills and alcohol to wind down. I had no idea yoga could help."

The phone inside the house rang and she excused herself.

"Are you a yoga devotee?" Ariel asked Kate.

"I'm afraid not. I can barely touch my toes." Kate's athletic endeavors had been limited to walking, gentle hikes, and snowshoeing. She couldn't do the last in Texas, but she had gone horseback riding once with Vivi.

Ariel laughed. "Me neither. But maybe I should give it a try." She glanced up as Bebe stormed back onto the porch. "What's the matter?"

Bebe clenched her fists and paced about. "I suppose I should put my money where my mouth is and do some deep breathing." She stopped and took a couple of slow breaths.

Kate felt a pang of fear. "It's not Martha, is it?"

Bebe shook her head, her fingers unfurling as she relaxed. "No. The group attending my retreat tomorrow canceled." She snapped her fingers. "Just like that. Out of the blue." She sank down into her chair and put her hands over her face. "I'm sunk before I even got started."

Ariel cocked her head to one side, frowning. After a minute, she said, "I'll ask my friends to come, if you want. But you'll have to wait until the weekend, if that's OK."

"You'd really do that for me?" Bebe put her hand to her chest. "This weekend would work. I have room for six."

"Five friends and me. That's six." Ariel shrugged one slim shoulder. "The women I'm thinking of are trendsetters, and they'll help you get the word out." Her full lips quirked. "I'm not totally being unselfish with this offer. I figure if I help you, you can help us promote the modeling agency. Then Derek can pay you back, and I can have a baby."

A succession of emotions ran over Bebe's face—surprise, gratitude, and a trace of pain. Her hands twisted together, the knuckles whitening.

Feeling intrusive, Kate averted her eyes. Had Bebe wanted children, perhaps? If so, it would be hard to watch it happen with her replacement.

But the older woman quickly rallied. "Of course I'll support the agency. How about offering a photography session for the women while they're here? It can be a paid option."

"Great idea. Those women would die to have their pictures taken by the famous Derek Morehouse." The two women shared a laugh, then fell silent.

After a moment, Kate asked, "Any word on Martha, how she's doing?"

Bebe's face lightened. "Yes, she's much better. I went to see her last night."

"Does she know who hit her?" Ariel's face twisted in sympathy.

Bebe shook her head. "No. She doesn't remember a thing. That's to be expected, I've heard, with that type of injury."

Kate thought about asking Bebe if she'd learned Martha's real name, but she wasn't sure how much she should say in front of Ariel. So she merely commented, "Vivi and I are going to visit her this afternoon."

"Say hello for me," Bebe said. "Tell her I'll be in again later tonight."

Ariel glanced at the wall clock. "I don't have a whole lot of time this morning, so we should probably do the measuring." Putting her cup on the table, she stood, and the others followed suit.

Inside the house, Bebe took them down the hallway past the spacious Victorian-furnished living room to the wardrobe room. The medium-size room basically served as a giant closet, housing half a dozen metal racks stuffed with gorgeous clothes, a couple of worktables, a sewing machine, a mirrored vanity set, and an ironing board. "You can work in here, Kate. Just clear off a table and set up your things. Once you're done with Ariel, I'll show you the crochet outfits." She left, shutting the door softly behind her.

Kate glanced around at the clothes, eager to get started. Judging by the sumptuous fabrics and rich colors, most of these garments were designer originals.

"I'm ready when you are."

Kate whirled around to see Ariel standing in her underwear. She didn't seem embarrassed in the least, and Kate had the sense such procedures were old hat for Ariel, which made sense. A human model was often called a mannequin, after all, and often functioned as a shapely rack to hang clothes upon. She quickly pulled out her notebook and pen and got to work.

"You probably think it's strange that Bebe and I get along so well," Ariel said.

Kate checked the length of Ariel's arm again. Sleeves that were too short were a pet peeve of hers. "No, I think it's great."

"She should hate me. I stole Derek from her."

Shock and distaste jolted Kate, and she dropped one end of the tape. What could she possibly say? Fortunately, Ariel continued speaking, not seeming to notice Kate's uneasiness. Maybe being measured was like going to your hairdresser—you could confide in someone paid to listen while performing such a personal service.

"She told me that it was over between them anyway, so she forgave me." Ariel gave a little bark of a laugh. "I never thought

I'd be friends with my husband's ex, but she's wonderful."

"She certainly seems to be," Kate agreed neutrally.

The model's flawless face darkened. "Maybe she was relieved. Derek is great in a lot of ways, but when it comes to money ... let's just say this modeling agency better pan out."

Kate finished measuring Ariel's inseam and rose to her feet. "With both of you involved, I'm sure it will." Rolling up the tape, she changed the subject hastily. "Thanks so much. I really appreciate you volunteering to be my fit model."

"No problem." Ariel slid one endless gam into the leg of her slacks. "I checked you out. You're good. I hope your editor will approve us doing the photography for the book."

"I hope so too." She made a note on her mental to-do list to call Alexus about their offer.

Kate was grateful she had a fit model available when she examined the crochet clothing Bebe chose from her collection. The blouses, cardigans, tops, skirts, and dresses were much finer in stitch and more elaborate in design than she expected. Her most advanced design skills would be needed for this project.

Kate fingered a cream-colored dress with a square neck, handkerchief hem, and angel sleeves. "This is so much prettier than what I usually think of '70s clothes."

"It wasn't all gaudy colors and macramé back then," Bebe said with a laugh. Holding a dress up by its hanger, she examined it with a cocked head. "But I'd forgotten how attractive they are."

"A lot of them have a flower motif, I notice." Kate traced the outline of an eight-petal blossom with a pinwheel center.

"A leftover from the flower children, I guess." Bebe hung the dress up. "Well, I'll get out of your hair and let you work." She moved toward the door.

"Bebe? Thanks again. Your collection is wonderful, and I really appreciate your help with this project."

Bebe waved a dismissive hand. "No problem. Call me if you need anything."

Kate spent a little time looking at the clothes, holding them up against her body, closely examining the crochet patterns and the garment construction. She took a deep breath, smiling in excitement. Visions of updated designs were already filtering into her mind. She could do this. Pulling out a sketch pad and grid, she got to work.

The sound of her cellphone ringing brought her out of her creative trance. It was Vivi. "What's up?"

"Can we push off meeting for a couple of hours? I've got another meeting with some prospective clients." She laughed. "Get this. It's an association of event planners holding a conference. Talk about stress!"

"They do sound like a tough group." Kate glanced at the time, noting with surprise that the morning had flown by. "If we meet later, I can stop by Once Upon a Yarn first. That'll be perfect." The needlecraft shop owned by her friend Paige Bryant was one of her favorite places in the city.

"I'll meet you there. Bye." Vivi signed off.

Sensing she'd come to a natural stopping place in her creative activity, Kate took photographs of several pieces for later reference, and then made a list of threads and trims to look for at the shop.

"How's it going?" Bebe popped her head around the doorway.

"Great." Kate tucked the sketch pad into her tote. "I'd like to come back another day this week to keep working, if that's all right."

"Anytime." She smiled. "It was a lot of fun looking at

those old clothes again. I can't wait to see your designs."

Bebe walked Kate out, and she headed back toward Fort Worth.

Kate easily found a parking space outside Once Upon a Yarn. As she grabbed her list and headed inside, her stomach rumbled. She'd have to grab something to eat soon. Working hard gave her an appetite.

"Hello, Kate," Paige called out as she entered the store. Paige, an attractive woman in her fifties, was stocking a display of pastel baby wool in the yarn section. "Would you like to join me for lunch? I've got chicken salad sandwiches on homemade wheat bread." Straightening, she brushed her strawberry-blond bob into place.

As though answering Paige, Kate's stomach rumbled again, and she laughed. "You read my mind. Or my stomach, rather. I'm starving."

Paige finished stocking the yarn and carried the empty box toward the storeroom. "We'll have to sit behind the counter. I'm all alone today."

She soon returned with paper plates of sandwiches and a couple of cans of soft drinks, and Kate joined her in the area usually reserved for employees. "Thanks. This looks great." The sandwich was heaped with chicken salad studded with nuts, grapes, and apples and topped with lettuce and tomato. She took a bite. "And it tastes great."

"Glad you like it," Paige said, taking a bite of her own sandwich. "So, what are you working on?" Paige's vivid green eyes danced. She loved hearing about Kate's designs and was one of her biggest supporters.

Between mouthfuls, Kate filled her in on the new book and Bebe's collection. After they finished eating, she put her phone on the counter and scrolled through the shots she had taken, while Paige made the appropriate "oohs" and "aahs."

"I used to wear things like this," Paige commented, "although I experienced the tail end of the '70s, of course." She winked. "Actually, Cheri might like these." Paige's daughter was a fashion-conscious teenager.

"That's what I'm hoping. Vanessa said '70s styles are coming back." She pulled her list out for Paige. "I want to buy threads and trims today so I can get started."

Paige ran her finger down Kate's list. "I've got plenty of that weight and color. And this one. Have you decided about other colors yet? I might have to make an order."

"I'm thinking of doing the collection in cream and pink. Maybe one garment in ecru. Period appropriate but also very today."

Paige nodded. "Oh, that sounds gorgeous. Those colors will really highlight the pattern design." The store's phone rang and Paige picked up, holding up a forefinger to indicate that Kate should wait.

"I can't that night," Paige said. "I've got a dinner party with friends." She smiled at Kate. "But how about the following evening? ... All right. I'll see you then. At seven." She hung up, making a rueful face. "I've just joined another committee." Paige had a caring heart and was often asked to help with charities.

"Patrick made me promise it would be the last one for a while." She shrugged. "But I couldn't say no. It's a women's shelter."

"For abused women?" Kate felt a shiver. She had had personal experience with domestic abuse.

Paige's pretty mouth turned down. "Yes, and some of the stories are heartbreaking. Especially when children are involved." She rustled around on the counter and found a brochure. "We're always looking for fundraising ideas. So if you think of something, let me know."

Kate studied the brochure. "Where is the shelter located?" There was only a phone number for contact information.

"It's secret. So the abusers can't find their victims." Paige shuddered. "So horrible." She picked up their empty paper plates, put them into the trash, and briskly rubbed her hands together, dismissing both stray crumbs and the topic of the shelter. "Let's go find what you need."

Kate slipped the brochure into her bag. Maybe Vivi would have some ideas about how the shelter could raise money. As Paige said, it was a worthy cause.

"Hey, you two." Kate and Paige turned to see Vivi pushing through the shop door, clutching a big arrangement of flowers in one arm.

"Hey yourself, Vivi." Paige paused from ringing up Kate's sizable purchase, which included cones of thread, ribbon in several widths, floral lace, and pom-pom edge trimming. "Nice flowers."

"Are those for Martha?" Kate asked. "Nice idea." She wished she'd thought of flowers.

"Yes." Vivi set the colorful arrangement of small sunflowers and daisies on the counter. "It's cheerful, isn't it? Guaranteed to make anyone feel better."

Paige looked puzzled. "Who's Martha?"

Vivi glanced at Kate. "You didn't tell her about all the excitement?" At Kate's headshake, she filled Paige in on the troubling events of the previous day.

In turn, Kate shared the news that Martha was using an alias. "Maybe they know who she really is by now," she concluded. "I haven't heard from Peter today to ask him."

"Maybe she's a criminal herself." Vivi's eyes gleamed with interest.

Paige rubbed her chin thoughtfully. "Maybe so. Just remember, crime isn't the only reason for someone to use a false identity."

"What do you mean, Paige?" Kate asked.

"Some of the women at the shelter change their identities before they leave. They have to so their exes can't find them."

"Do you think Paige is right?" Vivi asked as they trudged down the hospital corridor, their shoes squeaking on the shiny tile. She lowered her voice as they passed an orderly pushing a gurney. "Do you think Martha is hiding from someone?"

"Someone or something." Kate searched both sides of the hall for room 306, where the nurse had said Martha Brown was recovering. "It could explain why she was attacked." She tugged on Vivi's sleeve. "This way." They turned an elbow in the corridor and then made an immediate right into Martha's room.

A woman with her leg in traction occupied the bed by the window, eyes closed in apparent slumber. Curtains shrouded the closest bed, so Kate tiptoed up and pulled them slightly apart to peek through. Maybe Martha was napping too, in which case they would leave the flowers and go.

But instead of a dozing Martha, Kate discovered an empty bed.

Six

Kate crept away from the empty bed, resisting the urge to duck down and peek under it. "Martha's not there," she whispered to Vivi.

Vivi glanced at the adjoining bathroom door, which stood ajar. "Maybe she's in the restroom."

"I don't think so. The light is off."

"Maybe she's off having tests." Vivi set the flower arrangement on the bedside table. "Let's go ask the nurse."

At the nurses' station, they approached Carlos, who had directed them to Martha's room. He was sitting at a computer, entering information. "Excuse me," Kate said. "Martha's not in her room. Is she somewhere else in the hospital?"

His eyes widened in alarm. "Uh, not that I'm aware of." He swiveled in his seat and addressed another nurse. "Gloria. Ms. Brown in 306 didn't have any labs or X-rays this afternoon, did she?"

Gloria looked equally puzzled. "Not that I'm aware of."

Carlos tapped on the keys. "She didn't have anything scheduled." He swiveled again, his gaze meeting Gloria's. "I'll go check." He jumped up and darted around the station toward Martha's room, followed by Kate and Vivi.

He checked the bathroom, which was empty, and then the closet. That, too, was empty. Next he went to the lounge area—but no Martha. "Looks like Ms. Brown checked herself out," he said, trotting back toward the desk. "I'll call security."

Kate hoped Martha had left under her own steam and

that someone else hadn't taken her away. Stepping into the hallway, she quickly called Peter.

"Either she's afraid of someone or she's trying to evade the law herself," he said in response to the news.

"That's what I thought," Kate said. "Bebe called one of her job references. Maybe you could pick up the trail to her identity there."

"Good idea." He groaned. "I was hoping to see you later, but now I'll definitely be tied up."

"We have Paige's dinner party tomorrow night," she reminded him. "We'll see each other then, if you don't have to cancel."

He gave a big sigh. "I hope not. Anyway, I'll be over as soon as possible to interview the staff." He lowered his voice. "Why don't you wait there, and I'll take your statement?"

Kate's cheeks flushed at the insinuation in his tone. "Oh, detective, you make that sound like an intriguing proposition!"

"It is. See you soon."

Vivi gave her a smirk as she disconnected. "My my. Was that flirtatious banter I heard?"

Kate smiled. "I'm afraid so." While she was very concerned about Martha's well-being, she had to admit that working with Peter on cases was turning into a nice partnership with delightful fringe benefits.

That evening, Kate heated a bowl of leftover spaghetti and curled up in the living room to watch television. It seemed she'd hardly had any downtime lately, and taking an hour or two to zone out felt like an indulgence.

She was flicking through the channels when the news caught her eye. A newscaster with Texas-cheerleader good looks and big hair was standing in front of the hospital she had visited earlier. The tag line read, "Woman missing after assault." She quickly turned up the sound.

"Police tonight are searching for Martha Brown, fifty, who is missing from this Fort Worth hospital. Brown was assaulted yesterday at the Magnolia Creek farm owned by former supermodel Bebe Morehouse."

Kate groaned as one side of the screen filled with pictures of Bebe, past and present. Of course, a reporter had put two and two together after catching the police scanner and figuring out the significance of the 911 address. Once you were famous, any news that was even marginally related would inevitably trigger a mention. And of course, in this case, Bebe *was* involved since she owned the property.

Kate's stomach sank. *What if Bebe is a suspect?* True, she didn't really know the woman, but she liked her and had a hard time imagining that Bebe would attack someone in cold blood and leave her lying there. *Besides, what motive would she have?*

With an effort, she tuned back in to the news. "Ms. Brown was admitted to this hospital with a serious head injury." The reporter gestured to the building, which was illuminated by floodlights.

Kate's heart skipped a beat when the reporter turned slightly. "I've got Fort Worth Detective Peter Matthews here with me tonight." Peter came into view, brushing a hand through his unruly hair. "Tell me, detective, why are you concerned about Ms. Brown leaving the hospital?"

Peter looked very handsome on television and quite comfortable in front of the camera.

"Ms. Brown was still recovering from her injuries, so

we're concerned about her health and well-being," he said, his expression both sincere and authoritative. "Anyone who has seen Ms. Brown or has knowledge of her whereabouts should call us immediately."

An inset picture of Martha appeared on the screen. It was obviously from her driver's license, as she had the characteristic deer-in-the-headlights gaze, but her square face was attractive.

"Thank you, detective." The camera shifted so only the woman was on-screen. Kate muted the volume and grabbed her phone. Peter didn't pick up, so she left a message. "Hey there, TV star, it's your biggest fan. Just a quick question. Or comment, really. Please tell me Bebe isn't a suspect."

Kate knew full well the distress caused by being under suspicion. When she'd first moved to Fort Worth, her former publisher had been murdered, and for a while she'd been the prime suspect. It had been a grueling experience. To take her mind off bad memories and worrying about Martha, she went to her studio, hoping the absorbing task of designing would help settle her uneasiness. Nothing else she had ever attempted was able to so fully engage both the creative and the detail-oriented parts of her mind. Once in that zone, everything else simply disappeared.

As she sketched and counted under a circle of lamplight, she allowed the peace of the quiet night to seep into her frazzled nerves. By the time exhaustion made her eyes droop, she had made significant progress on the first piece, a sleeveless camisole blouse that would look equally good with a full skirt, a denim mini, or a suit. She was excited to see how it would look. But that was a project for another day.

The design work did the trick, and Kate enjoyed a restful night's sleep. She got up a little earlier than usual, eager to get on the road back to the farm before the workmen showed up. The jackhammering appeared to be over, but the digging equipment was still parked outside, ready to rip into the soil.

Feeling the need for a substantial breakfast, she put water in the microwave for poached eggs and slipped two pieces of bread into the toaster. The timer on the microwave and her phone on the counter rang at the same time. Ignoring the boiling water for a moment, she grabbed the phone, hoping it was Peter.

Vivi's smiling face was on the screen. "Good morning," she said. "I have the day off. Want to do something?"

Kate glanced at the clock with a laugh. "Why aren't you still in bed? That's what I'd be doing on *my* day off." She opened the fridge and grabbed two eggs.

Vivi yawned. "I know. I should be, but I'm too wired, thinking about Martha. I checked the news, and they haven't found her yet."

After opening the microwave door, Kate cracked the eggs and slipped them into the water. "That's terrible. I hope she's not in worse shape than when we saw her last." She shut the door and set the timer. "I'm going out to the farm to look at Bebe's collection again. Want to ride along?"

"I'd love to. Maybe we can find out more about who Martha really is and help track her down that way." She yawned again. "Oh, did I tell you? Bebe called and asked me to help her with the retreat. As a side job."

"That's cool, but will your boss mind?" The timer dinged again. "Let me put you down for a minute. I'm handling hot water." She set the phone down and pulled a pair of oven mitts out of a drawer. Then she carefully took the bowl of water out of the microwave and set it on the counter. After one minute, the eggs were cooked the way she liked them: whites firm and yolks runny.

"What are you doing?" Vivi asked when Kate picked up the phone again.

Kate explained while buttering toast. She pulled the eggs out of the water with a slotted spoon and set them on top of the toast. "Perfectly poached every time."

"That sounds great. Oh, and my boss doesn't care as long as it's not for a competitor. And the side work doesn't cut into my hours for him." Vivi laughed. "I've increased event revenue by 25 percent over last year already. They love me."

"You're the best, Vivi." Kate stared at the steaming eggs, mouth watering. "I've got to eat these eggs before they get cold. Come over as soon as you're ready."

Within an hour, just as truckloads of orange-vested men in hard hats arrived in the neighborhood, Kate and Vivi left for the farm. They were creeping along Magnolia Creek's bumper-to-bumper Main Street when Peter finally called. "Grab that, will you, Vivi? I'd better not."

"Hello, Peter. … No, you don't have the wrong number. This is Vivi." She winked at Kate. "What's that? Let me put you on speakerphone."

"Hi, Peter," Kate called. "We're in traffic. On the way to the farm." She kept her eyes fixed on the stop-and-go traffic ahead.

Peter cleared his throat. "Sorry. Frog in my throat. I was up almost all night."

Kate's heart gave a thump. "Did you find her?" She prayed that, if so, the woman was all right.

Peter let out a sigh of discouragement. "Nope. Not yet. I wanted to answer the question you left me on voice mail last night. Bebe isn't a suspect. Fortunately for her, she was on the telephone during the whole window when Martha could have been injured. Her tech guy vouched for her."

"Wow," Vivi said, her eyes wide. "Being stuck on the phone with tech support actually paid off for once."

Peter laughed. "Good point. Anyway, I won't keep you. I've got to get some sleep. I have a dinner date tonight."

"That's right, *we* do," Kate teased him with a start of pleasure. "I'm looking forward to it."

"Pick you up at six?"

"Sounds good," Kate said, raising her voice over Vivi's whistles and hoots while waving at her to be quiet. "Please let me know if you hear anything about Martha." Once he hung up, Kate gave Vivi a mock scowl. "You're too much. Next time Sam calls you, I'm going to make a big song and dance about it." Vivi occasionally dated Texas Ranger Sam Tennyson.

"*If* he calls." Vivi's lower lip pushed out in a pout. "I haven't heard from him in over two weeks."

Traffic finally cleared and Kate pressed the gas. She threw a glance at her friend. "But I thought he was the serious one and *you* wanted to play it cool."

Vivi shrugged and turned to watch the passing scenery. "That's true. But now that *he's* playing it cool, I don't like it."

Kate hid a smile. No doubt Sam was using Vivi's own medicine on her, and it appeared to be working. "I have an idea. Why don't we have a cookout at my house soon? That'll give you an excuse to call Sam."

Vivi's mouth dropped open. "You think I should call him?"

"Why not? It's the twenty-first century. Women call men all the time."

Her friend's voice was a low mumble as she studied her hands clasped on her lap. "What if he says no?"

"He won't." The tall, handsome ranger positively vibrated with delight and interest whenever he was around Vivi. "And if he does, so what? He's just one of a million fish in the sea."

"You're not helping, Kate." A small smile curved Vivi's lips. "Maybe I will give him a shout. It can't hurt, right?" She was silent for a moment. "My mother has a great recipe for a brisket rub. Real Texas style."

"That sounds great," Kate said. "I love brisket." They spent the rest of the trip discussing the menu for the barbecue. According to Vivi, acceptable sides included beans, coleslaw, and Texas toast.

"What on earth is she doing?" Vivi asked as they pulled into the driveway at the farm. On a patch of grass in front of the house, Bebe balanced on her forearms with her legs curved forward, almost touching her forehead. Tansy, Bebe's pet hen, pecked around the grass nearby.

"It looks like very advanced yoga." Kate parked the car while Vivi craned to watch the model as she moved into another pose, this one a headstand.

"I'll say. The women who come to the retreat will get their money's worth, all right."

"I couldn't do that if I tried," Kate said ruefully. "And I'm younger than she is."

They climbed out and slammed the van's doors. "You're amazing," Vivi called out as they approached.

Bebe relaxed onto her back and then sprang to her feet. She picked up a towel and wiped her face. "I've been doing yoga for thirty years." She grinned. "First to get in shape, then to relax, and now to make money. I hope." She slung the towel over her arm and walked toward the house, Tansy at her heels. "Would you two like coffee? And I've got fresh strawberries and yogurt, both locally sourced."

"I'd love coffee," Kate said.

"I already had breakfast, but I could definitely use a snack." Vivi patted her slender midriff. "They're low calorie, right?"

"Yes. I try to cut calories where I can, but you do need a little fat in your diet, you know." Bebe gestured toward the porch chairs. "Have a seat, and I'll be out in a few minutes."

"I feel like putting myself under her tutelage," Vivi said. "I'd really get in shape." She rocked the chair vigorously. "This is about all the exercise I'll manage today. I do run around the hotel. I wonder if that counts."

"Of course it does. I should walk more often myself. I sit too much." Kate glanced around for the hen to be sure the rockers didn't hit her. "Where's Tansy?"

"She's over there." Vivi nodded toward the end of the porch where Tansy was investigating a potted plant. "That chicken acts like a dog the way she follows Bebe around."

Kate relaxed for a moment, enjoying the early morning sun and the hen's amusing antics. Their hostess soon appeared with a tray carrying coffee and attractive parfait glasses of yogurt and berries.

"Now I wish *I'd* asked for some," Kate said.

Bebe half rose. "I can fix you one."

Kate waved her down. "Please don't bother. My eyes are bigger than my stomach."

"I heard they haven't found Martha yet," Bebe said after a few minutes. "I'm really worried about her."

"Me too," Kate said. "She didn't know anyone else in the area, did she?"

Bebe took a sip of coffee, her gaze distant as she considered the question. "I don't think so. I put the ad online and she answered it by email. Her résumé said she was from Houston."

Kate remembered her mentioning that before. "Did

you check her references?" Kate hoped Bebe had spoken to someone who knew Martha.

"That's what the police wanted to know." She wrinkled her nose in a grimace. "I felt like they were blaming her for the assault. Not impressed."

"It's not that," Kate assured her. "Martha Brown isn't her real name."

Bebe's eyes widened, and the coffee mug almost slipped out of her hand. "What are you talking about?" Managing to hold onto the cup, she set it on the table beside her.

Kate explained what Peter had told her, that Martha Brown was using a false identification. "It's important to find people who know her so they can pick up the trail."

"*That's* why they wanted her résumé. I wondered." The older woman still looked stunned as she tried to absorb the fact that she'd hired someone operating under a false identity. She shook her head. "I can't believe it. She was so sweet." She frowned, perplexed. "She could be anyone. How could I be so foolish?"

"Maybe she's in some kind of trouble," Vivi said. "Not everyone with a fake ID is a criminal."

"If someone wants to disappear, surely that's up to them," Kate said. "But in this case, she's injured, and the police are hoping to find out who assaulted her."

"The person who hit her might have taken her from the hospital." Vivi's face was grim. "Her life may be at risk."

Bebe put her hand to her mouth and moaned. "Oh, I hope not." Tears sprang to her eyes. "Poor … Martha. I guess she'll always be Martha to me."

Kate glanced at Vivi. "We'd like to see her résumé, if that's OK. The police are great and all, but we sometimes find things they miss."

Bebe slowly rose to her feet. "I'll go get it. It's in my office."

"That really upset her," Vivi said after Bebe had gone into the house. "Maybe we shouldn't have told her."

"I hated to tell her, but she needed to know the truth. Otherwise, she might fail to mention an important clue, something that she doesn't even realize *is* important." Kate took a last sip of cold coffee.

Vivi laughed. "I think I understood that last sentence." She glanced toward the driveway. "It looks like Bebe has a visitor."

The vehicle was behind the trees, but its loud, rumbling engine could be clearly heard as it groaned along the lane. A giant Humvee came into view, its glossy black paint glistening in the sun.

"Gosh, could they make it any bigger?" Vivi's tone was scornful. "I wonder how much gas that thing burns? One mile per gallon maybe?"

"I guess whoever owns it probably has enough money that they don't care." Kate jumped to her feet. "What the heck is he doing?"

Even though Kate's van was parked properly off to the side, the driver of the enormous vehicle was having trouble navigating the limited space. While she stared in horror, expecting to hear the crunch of her fender any second, the Hummer swung to the right instead and took out a section of fence. The huge tires rolled over it with a cracking of wood and then ground to a halt.

Vivi gasped. "I can't believe he did that."

"I know. I thought he was going to hit my van for sure." Kate stared at the windshield, trying to see the driver, but only a hat and sunglasses were visible. The side windows were tinted, she noticed.

Bebe appeared on the porch, clutching a manila folder in

her hand. With an exclamation of anger, she set it on the table beside the tray and ran down the steps, waving her hands.

The passenger door opened and a heavyset man wearing a ten-gallon hat and cowboy boots slid to the ground. As he hitched up his pants, which were adorned with a huge silver belt buckle, Kate recognized him from the newspaper. It was Slim Baker, the owner of the proposed motor sports park. "Slim" was obviously an ironic nickname. Even his fingers were fat little sausages. A diamond pinky ring sparkled on his right hand as he reached back into the vehicle and pulled out an envelope, then slammed the door. He tucked the envelope into his shirt pocket.

Bebe folded her arms across her chest. "What do you want, Slim? And you're going to pay for my fence, by the way."

Slim merely smirked and sauntered toward her, swinging his arms like a cowboy in a gunfight. He caught sight of Kate and Vivi watching from the porch and mimed a tip of his hat as his beady eyes flickered over them.

"I don't like him," Vivi whispered.

Kate didn't either, despite the ingratiating smile he aimed at Bebe. "Hello there, little lady. How are you today?" He continued to grin, resting both hands on his hips as if he had all day to chat.

"I'll be a lot better once you're off my property."

He held up one meaty hand. "Hold on, hold on. You're going to want to listen to what I have to say." He reached for the envelope. "I'm fixing to buy your farm."

Bebe stamped her foot. "What? Over my dead body. You're not getting this farm. It's been in my family for a hundred years." She shook her head, her long hair flying about her shoulders.

Vivi nudged Kate. "Look." Kate followed her gaze to the Hummer. Tansy had flown to the roof and was now pecking around, investigating and no doubt scratching the glossy finish.

Slim looked around the grounds, sneering. "And look at what your family has done with the place." He held out the envelope. "I've got an offer, in writing. For today only. Time-limited, so you ought to take a look at it, little lady." He flapped the envelope at her.

"The answer is no. I don't care how much you offer. Now get off my property." She raised her arm and pointed belligerently at the portly Slim. "And quit calling me 'little lady.'"

Seeming to enjoy the conflict, he waved the envelope again. "I'm not leaving until you take this, so you might as well."

She snatched it from his grasp and immediately dropped it. For good measure, she stepped on it and pressed it into the ground. "Are you happy now? Get lost."

He tipped his hat again. "You'll want to be reading that." Moving slowly, he turned and ambled back toward the Hummer. Bebe stood watching as he climbed in and gently closed the door. The engine roared to life, and the chicken squawked and flew off the roof, landing in the garden. She ran toward her owner.

"Look what she did!" Vivi stifled a laugh. A telltale streak of white marred the Hummer's flawless black finish.

Somehow the driver managed to get the beast turned around and headed back toward the road without causing further damage. As soon as it disappeared into the trees, Bebe came back to the porch. By her crossed arms and angry expression, Kate guessed she was still fuming. The envelope still lay on the grass. After a cursory peck or two at it, Tansy moved on to root for worms in a loamy flower bed.

"Tansy left Slim a little gift," Vivi said as Bebe climbed the steps.

Her face lightened a trace. "What?" She sank down into a rocker.

"She decided to ... ah ... express her feelings on top of the Hummer," Kate said.

Bebe finally caught on and burst into laughter, joined by Kate and Vivi.

"I know I shouldn't let him get to me," Bebe said after the merriment died down. "I vow not to. Then when I'm around him, I just lose it."

"I don't blame you," Vivi said. "He's creepy."

"And rude," Kate said. "He was insulting your lovely property. I wanted to tell him off myself."

"I'm not selling. I wish he'd get it through his thick head. I'm not going to allow them to build that horrible, tacky motor sports park either. It would ruin this whole area." She rocked back and forth, pensive. "Well, I should let you get to work, Kate. Vivi, you feel like discussing the retreat schedule?"

"I'd love to," Vivi said. She pulled out her tablet from her purse. "I have an agenda template we can use to block out what you've planned so far. Then we can work on the rest of the schedule."

"Are you going to have other activities besides yoga classes?" Kate asked. "Forgive my ignorance. I've never been to a yoga retreat."

"The whole purpose is to help people learn to relax and take better care of themselves. Besides yoga, I offer meditation, prayer time, and plain old free time to relax." Her eyes lit up. "I have an idea. Do you teach classes, Kate?"

"Sometimes. What do you have in mind?"

"How about offering a crochet class? I like to knit myself, and I know crafts are both practical and relaxing. I think some of my guests would benefit from slowing down to work with their hands."

"I can do that." Kate enjoyed teaching others the skill

she loved. "I'll come up with a couple of ideas for small, easy items they can make quickly."

Vivi made an entry on her tablet. "What time do you think, Bebe?"

Kate left the two of them discussing the scheduled events and went inside to study the vintage garments again. Photographs were useful, but they were no substitute for seeing the patterns in person. Once again she lost herself in designing, allowing inspiration to spool into her mind like a dream she could reach out and grasp.

"Kate." Vivi's arrival in the doorway startled her. "Sorry to interrupt, but this is important. Bebe just received a threatening letter."

Seven

Kate put aside her sketch pad and hurried after Vivi to the porch. Bebe sat in a rocker, moving slowly back and forth as she stared at a piece of paper in her lap. The discarded envelope lay on the floor.

"Can I take a look at it?" Kate pulled her sleeve down over her hand so as not to leave any fingerprints.

"Sure, go ahead. It's probably just someone's idea of a joke." Bebe handed the letter to Kate.

"You'll regret your decision" was typed on plain white paper. Kate flipped it over. Nothing else was written on it.

"This is wonderfully vague," Kate said. "Although it probably has to do with you refusing to sell the property."

"That's certainly a possibility." Bebe reached for the envelope. "But this has a Fort Worth postmark, so it was mailed before Slim Baker showed up and made his latest offer."

Careful not to touch the envelope, Vivi leaned over and examined the postmark. "She's right. This was mailed yesterday."

Kate sat on the wicker sofa, carefully placing the letter on the surface. "We really need to put them both in a plastic bag for the police."

Bebe shook her head. "I don't want to bother the police with this. It's probably a crank letter. I've gotten more than my share, believe me."

"So have I," Kate said. "Calls and letters. Usually someone was trying to scare me off an investigation."

"Did they succeed?" Bebe asked, raising an eyebrow.

Vivi answered for Kate. "No. If anything, it made her more determined."

Bebe waved her hand. "There's your answer then. I don't regret any decisions I've made, so I'll just have to live with the consequences."

Kate hoped those consequences wouldn't turn deadly, but she didn't press the issue further. "Let's just put these somewhere safe anyway. Then when—*if* anything else happens, the clues will be intact."

"I'll go along with that." Bebe picked up the folder with Martha's résumé and pulled it out. "Why don't you put them in here?" She handed the résumé to Vivi. "You can keep this. I've already made another copy."

"Thanks. We'll call these places later and see what we can find out." Vivi gave the résumé to Kate, and she slid it into her tote before putting the threat and envelope into the folder.

Bebe rose to her feet, taking the folder Kate handed to her. "I'm just about to have some lunch. Avocado-and-cheese sandwiches. Would you like to join me?"

"That sounds wonderful," Kate said. "Next time it's our treat, OK? We'll take you out."

"I like feeding people." Bebe paused in the doorway. "But now that you mention it, I do love Chop and Chips in Fort Worth."

"That's my favorite restaurant!" Vivi exclaimed. "We'll go there soon."

"So, what do you think about that threat?" Vivi asked Kate after their hostess had disappeared inside the house.

"If it weren't for the postmark, I'd be convinced that Slim left it. But it could also be from the woman she fired, Phoebe Newland."

"That's true." Vivi tapped her chin, thinking. "But maybe Slim knew she would turn him down."

"He'd have to be pretty certain. Can you imagine if it arrived after she said yes?" In Kate's experience, threats meant you were treading on someone's toes. In Bebe's case, there was a whole shoe store of candidates. Slim and Phoebe, for sure. But she was also dealing with her ex-husband and his new wife. And then there was Martha's unknown assailant.

Since the weather was so nice, Bebe served lunch under a vine-draped pergola in the garden. There weren't any blooms yet, but the lush leaves provided dappled shade and some protection from the surprisingly hot sun.

"I still can't get over how nice March is here," Kate said. "Back in Maine, they're dealing with a late-season snowstorm today." Earlier, she'd gotten a good-humored complaint about the weather via email from her good friend, Alice MacFarlane Parker.

"Ugh," Vivi said. "I only like snow for about five minutes at Christmas. On television."

Bebe inquired about Kate's background as well as Vivi's, seeming genuinely interested and asking lots of questions. After that topic was exhausted, the conversation turned to the retreat.

"All of Ariel's friends confirmed, so we're all set there," Bebe said. "The main room in the barn where we have the classes needs painting, though. And guess what? The contractor isn't coming." She curled her lips in a scowl. "He said someone from here canceled the job. I certainly didn't, so I think the screwup is on his end."

Kate glanced at Vivi and could tell by her wide eyes that she was also putting two and two together. The website hacking, retreat cancellations, and now a contractor dropping out. Bebe appeared to be suffering from a pattern of harassment.

Now wasn't the time to discuss it. "Is it a complicated job?" Kate asked Bebe. Maybe they could find someone to do it, even on short notice.

"No, not really. I had the walls patched, so there are splotches of gray everywhere. I just need someone to roll on a couple of coats of paint."

"Isn't Vanessa looking for extra money?" Vivi asked Kate.

"That's right. Vanessa is my college-age daughter," she explained to Bebe. "She helped me paint the inside of my house. She would do a great job."

"I'll bet some of her friends will help too," Vivi said. "All that youth and energy will get the job done in a hurry."

"That sounds like a good solution. Please ask her and let me know." Bebe gave a huge sigh. "Maybe this thing will pull together after all, despite all the roadblocks."

Kate's eyes met Vivi's again in understanding before Kate changed the subject. "What did you two decide on for a final agenda?"

Vivi gave the rundown of the slots for yoga, nutrition classes, meals, Kate's crochet class, the photography sessions with Derek, and free time.

"I'll make light and healthy meals," Bebe said, "and then explain how my guests can make better food choices at home and on the go."

"Get this." Vivi put a hand on Kate's elbow. "At the end of the retreat, we're going to have partner yoga. All the guests are married women, so Bebe is inviting their husbands on the last day for a class."

Kate imagined Peter in one of the pretzel poses Bebe had modeled earlier. "I'd like to see that."

Vivi laughed. "Me too. And we might get an opportunity." She nodded at Bebe. "You tell her."

"I'd like both of you to come and stay during the retreat," she said. "You'll need to be here for your class anyway, Kate, and Vivi is going to help me with logistics for the weekend—fortunately, since I don't have an assistant right now."

"I actually have the weekend free," Vivi said, "the only one from now until things slow down again in early November."

"I'd love to stay," Kate said, "especially since they're ripping up the street outside my house and I can't work there right now." Being away from her studio had been manageable for a couple of days, but it would be another week or two before the noisy tasks were done. Staying at the farm was a perfect alternative.

"Come stay now if you want," Bebe said, "both of you. I have plenty of room."

"I think I'll take you up on that," Kate said.

"Thanks so much," Vivi added.

Kate felt a swell of gratitude at Bebe's generous offer. Plus, if she stayed at the farm, she could keep an eye on Bebe and make sure someone didn't follow up on the threat in a more physical way.

A terrible idea flashed through her mind. *What if Bebe was the target of the attack on Martha?* The thought rooted and grew into a horrible certainty that made her blood run cold. Both women were tall and pretty, close in age, with long blond hair.

Bebe's life was in danger. She could feel it in her bones.

Although the dinner at Paige's wasn't formal, Kate decided to wear a flowing floral skirt, a sheer silk blouse, and a gossamer crocheted shawl with metallic threads to make the occasion feel special. She and Peter hadn't spent much time together lately, especially since the assault on Martha, and then her disappearance was added to his roster. Tonight was their chance to reconnect.

She smiled at herself in the mirror as she applied a light spritz of perfume. *I must be getting better. It wasn't that long ago that I wouldn't even dream of connecting with another man.* After her disastrous marriage, she had been the poster child for once bitten, twice shy. Perching on the bed, she pulled on glossy knee-high boots that looked great under the full skirt. One more twirl in front of the mirror and she was ready.

Peter was exactly on time, a trait she appreciated. She also appreciated the admiring look he gave her when she opened the door.

"You look lovely."

"Thank you, Peter." She grabbed her handbag and glanced around to make sure everything was in order before leaving.

He gestured to the jeans he wore with a sport jacket and cowboy boots, as usual. "Should I have dressed up?"

"I just felt like—how do you say it in Texas?—puttin' on the dog." Locking the door, she added, "Besides, you look good in jeans."

He ushered her toward the passenger side of his battered green Ford pickup. He pulled open the door for her and made a mock bow. "Your chariot awaits, dear lady." He winked.

Gathering her skirt, Kate climbed the high step with Peter's assistance, grateful for his thoughtful attention. He closed the door gently, then strode to the driver's side and got in. As he started the engine, Kate noticed he'd set the radio to an easy listening station.

She thought about asking him for an update on the case

but quickly pushed that idea aside. Instead, she leaned back against the wide cushioned seat and enjoyed the drive—city lights, moon rising above the tall buildings downtown, and a handsome man by her side.

Lights streamed from Paige's two-story Colonial, creating a welcoming sight as they pulled into the driveway. Accent lights also brightened the shrubbery and ornamental trees in the yard and outlined the walkway. Peter hopped out and opened Kate's door for her. They walked arm in arm to the front porch, and Peter rang the bell.

Paige flung the door open after a moment. "Come on in," she said with a wide smile. She gave them both a hug before leading them to the comfortable living room where her husband sat by the gas fireplace. "Patrick will get you a glass of wine while I finish up in the kitchen." Patrick, a handsome man with salt-and-pepper hair and wire-rimmed glasses, set aside his newspaper and rose to his feet as they entered.

"Do you need help?" Kate asked.

"No thanks. Everything is almost ready. Make yourself comfortable." Paige bustled away toward the back of the house.

"Kate. Peter. Welcome." Patrick hugged Kate and shook hands with Peter and then ushered them to seats on the upholstered sofa. "Red or white?" He moved to a buffet that held several bottles of wine.

"I'll take white," Kate said, and Peter concurred. After Patrick brought them their glasses, he poured himself one and sat down again.

"This is nice," Kate said, reaching her hands out to the fire. Even though the days were warm, March nights were still quite cool.

"It's just enough to take the evening chill off," Patrick agreed. "How have you been?"

The trio caught up, with Patrick sharing developments in the oil business where he worked as an executive. Moving from that topic, Peter asked, "So, what do you think about the Cowboys' lineup this year?"

Kate suppressed a smile. So many Texas conversations started with or led to two particular topics: oil and football.

Before Patrick could answer, Paige appeared in the doorway. "Dinner is served." She smiled at her husband. "I could use a hand for a minute."

He got right to his feet. "Absolutely, honey." Kate noticed again how well Paige and Patrick functioned as a couple. They'd been married for thirty years, which had surprised her when she learned their two children were teenagers, but they had managed to retain the consideration and closeness of young love.

Kate and Peter settled themselves across from each other in the cozy, candlelit dining room. Patrick entered holding a platter with four tiny Cornish hens, followed by Paige, who was carrying bowls of steaming mashed potatoes and green peas. On the table already were dishes of cranberry jelly, butter, and gravy, and a bowl of green salad.

"This looks fantastic, Paige," Kate said. She took a deep breath. The meal smelled wonderful too.

"It sure does." Peter unrolled the cloth napkin and spread it over his lap. "Nothing like a home-cooked meal."

Paige shrugged off the compliments. "I love to cook. Now dig in." Paige took her seat at the head of the table and passed the bowl of potatoes to Kate. Patrick served them each a hen and then took his own seat. After everyone had filled their plates, he said grace.

"Where are the kids tonight?" Kate asked once they had begun to eat.

"Bud is working and Cheri is at a friend's house." Paige laughed. "I used to long for a civilized dinner hour when they were small. Now the house seems so empty. They're always busy."

"I know what you mean," Kate said. "I still miss Vanessa."

"Is she enjoying Regency?" As an alumnus, Patrick was a dedicated proponent of the small college's excellence.

Kate gave him the rundown of Vanessa's class schedule. It was the perfect opportunity to mention her daughter's desire for more employment. "Paige, if you ever need a part-time employee, please consider Vanessa. She's always looking for more income. In fact, I've got to call her about a painting job at Bebe Morehouse's farm."

"Ooh, Bebe Morehouse." Paige's eyes lit up. "You remember Bebe Morehouse, don't you, dear?" Her tone was teasing. "He used to have one of her posters on his dorm room wall," she told the others.

Patrick pushed his glasses up with his thumb. "It was required study for our anatomy class." His deadpan tone made them all burst out laughing. "So, what's this about her farm? I didn't know she lived around here."

Kate explained her project and the great fun she was having using the vintage clothing as inspiration. "She has a lot more than the crocheted clothing." She shook her head in bemusement. "I saw clothes by Diane Von Furstenberg, Vivienne Westwood, Pucci, and Halston."

"I don't know who they are but they sound impressive," Peter said.

"Oh, they're impressive all right." Paige's eyes glowed. "All top designers. They must be gorgeous."

"They are. Silk, fur, leather … even gold and silver lamé. The '70s had some really wild clothes."

Patrick tugged on the sleeves of his neat cashmere sweater. "Maybe I should break out my old Nehru jacket and bell-bottoms."

"You wore bell-bottoms?" Kate couldn't imagine the conservative manager in such attire. "Did you have long hair too?"

Patrick nodded. "Yes, believe it or not. And a lot more of it." He chuckled.

"I'll show you some pictures," Paige said. "Such fun." She put a finger to her lips in a gesture Kate recognized. Paige had just gotten a brainstorm. "I have an idea. How about holding a vintage fashion show to benefit the women's shelter? Do you think Bebe would go for it?"

"I'll ask her. We'd have to be really careful with the clothes. I'm sure they're valuable."

"If you and I are in charge, we can make sure they're handled correctly. I think a fashion show could raise a lot of money." She beamed at Kate. "I knew we'd come up with a fundraising idea."

Without even being sure of how it had happened or what she was doing, Kate was suddenly managing a volunteer project. Oh well, it was for a very worthy cause. And it would probably be a great deal of fun. Maybe Vanessa and her friends could be the models. They were petite enough to fit into the vintage clothes.

Patrick correctly interpreted the stunned surprise Kate felt. "My wife strikes again." He shook his head. "You always amaze me, honey, how you get things done." Picking up the salad bowl, he asked, "Anyone want more salad?"

After dinner, they enjoyed tiramisu and decaf coffee in front of the fire while they played an entertaining new word game. When the mantel clock struck ten, Kate and Peter bade farewell with thanks and promises to get together again soon.

"What a nice night," Kate said as Peter drove toward home. "I like Paige and Patrick so much. Maybe I should invite them to the barbecue Vivi and I are planning."

"Barbecue?" Peter's brows rose. "I like the sound of that."

"Hopefully Sam Tennyson will too. That's why we're having it, to try to nudge things along for him and Vivi."

"Sounds—" Peter's phone rang. "Sorry. I better take this." He pulled over and spoke briefly into the phone before hanging up. "Sorry," he said again, signaling to pull back onto the highway. He sighed. "Another lead on Martha Brown's whereabouts just fizzled."

"That's too bad." Kate had deliberately not discussed the case all evening so they could enjoy the company of their friends and just feel like a couple on a date. But the call broke the spell, and all her thoughts and concerns came rushing back. "Peter, a couple of odd things happened today." She went on to tell him about Slim Baker's visit and the threat Bebe had received in the mail. "I had the strangest thought afterward. What if Bebe was the intended target, not Martha? They're similar in height, hair color, and build."

Peter ran his hand through his hair, a gesture that meant he was considering her theory. "That's an interesting idea, especially in light of Bebe getting a threatening letter. But then why is Martha missing?"

Eight

The lovely dinner she'd eaten sat heavy in Kate's stomach as she considered Peter's words. Whether Martha was the intended victim or not, the fact remained that living under a false identity and disappearing out of a hospital room were both troubling.

An idea flickered in her mind, sparked by the discussion she'd had with Paige about her work with the shelter. What if Martha was on the run from someone she knew? Being a battered girlfriend or wife would explain her actions. She could even be at the shelter right now. With their policy of nondisclosure for resident safety, she would be shielded from discovery by her attacker *and* the police.

Kate sighed. This theory brought Martha back front and center as the intended victim at the farm.

Peter glanced over. "That was a big sigh."

"I have to admit it. I'm confused." This case was incredibly complex, and she needed more information to sort it out. She'd call places on Martha's résumé as a start.

"You're not the only one. I'm baffled too, especially with the new information you just gave me." Peter slowed and turned into Kate's drive, the headlights sweeping over the front of her house. Good. She'd remembered to leave the living room lights on as well as the one over the front door.

He put the truck in park and then got out and came around to open her door. "I had a very nice time tonight, Kate." His smile was wide and sincere. "We've got to go out more often."

She slid out of the truck with Peter's assistance, gazing up at him. "Do you want to come in?" Part of her—a big part—wanted him to say yes, but actually she was so tired she was longing for her bed. And she'd be up early to move herself out to the farm the next day. She had a lot to do to get ready.

With a stab of disappointment, she saw him shake his head. Now he sighed, a deep gust of regret. "I'd love to. But I have to check in at the station right now, believe it or not. Not for the Martha case, another one that's heating up."

She stepped away from the truck, and he shut the passenger door behind her. "Gosh, it never ends for you, does it?" With his schedule, it was a miracle they *ever* got together.

"That's one of the reasons I never ..." He broke off, staring down at his feet.

Kate's spine tingled. She had a feeling the end of that sentence might be "got married." She reached out and touched his arm. "I understand. Oh, I wanted to tell you, I'm going to stay at the farm for a few days starting tomorrow to help with the retreat and work on my book. I didn't want you to think I disappeared too."

Lifting his head, he smiled. "Thanks for letting me know. I would have been worried if I came by and you were gone." He put an arm around her shoulders and they strolled toward the house.

Kate lowered her voice to a husky whisper. "You'd be concerned?" To her own amazement, she found herself batting her eyelashes. Good grief, was she flirting?

He leaned closer, his own voice low. "Of course, silly. I worry about you all the time." They stepped up onto her small front porch.

"Really, Mr. Policeman?" Her tone was teasing. Vanessa

had called law enforcement officers Mr. and Mrs. Policeman when she was small.

He gathered her in his arms with a groan. "Not as a policeman. As a ..." His voice trailed off. Perhaps not ready to declare anything—or sensing she wasn't ready, either—he kissed her instead. A tender, warm one. He pulled back with a grin. "Good night, Kate. I'll call you tomorrow."

"And I'll keep you posted if I learn anything more about Martha or Bebe." She paused, thinking of something. "By the way, there's a couples' yoga class during the retreat. Would you like to come?"

He threw back his head and laughed. "Me? Yoga?" He squeezed her shoulder, his big hand warm on her skin, and winked. "Maybe I will. But only for you."

"I'll hold you to that." Digging out her keys from her bag, she unlocked the door and went in. Once safely inside, she turned the locks, then went to the front window to watch as Peter loped back to the truck and jumped in. He backed out of the driveway and roared off into the night, intent on his next task.

What a wonderful night, Kate thought as she turned away from the window, slipping the shawl off her shoulders. *And what a wonderful man!*

Kate rose before sunrise, eager to pack and get on with her day and the move to the farm. At about seven, in the middle of packing clothing, she was surprised to hear her phone ring and even more amazed when she saw it was her daughter.

"Morning, Vanessa." Holding the phone to her ear, she

folded a pair of jeans and placed them in the suitcase. "You're up early."

Vanessa yawned. "I know. I have my one early class this morning. Remind me not to sign up for this slot next semester."

Kate laughed. "I'm getting a flashback to all those cold mornings when you didn't want to get up for school." In addition to not being a morning person, Vanessa hated getting out of bed in the winter, preferring to stay warm and snug under the quilts.

"At least we don't have below-zero weather here." She yawned again. "Anyway, I saw your text from last night. What's up?"

Kate opened her shirt drawer and selected both long- and short-sleeve tops. The weather in March could go from hot to cold, often over the course of the same day. "A couple of things. First, would you like to do a painting job out at Bebe Morehouse's farm? It's short notice, but Bebe needs it done before the yoga retreat. Her contractor bailed on her at the last minute."

"I'd love to. If she needs a crew, I bet my roommates will help. They're dying to meet Bebe."

"Great. I'll find out today about getting the supplies and tools you'll need." She placed the shirts on top of the jeans and tucked them in place. "I'm going to be staying at the farm for a few days." She explained why and the timeline.

"You're so lucky you get to stay out there. It sounds really cool." A thump indicated that Vanessa had climbed out of bed. "My roommate Zoe wants to be a model. Do you think she can get some pointers from Bebe?"

"Maybe. I'll ask." She opened her underwear drawer, half-thinking about the socks and stockings she'd need with the shoes she was taking. "Vanessa, what do you wear to a yoga class?"

"You're taking yoga?" She laughed. By the rustling Kate could hear, it sounded like Vanessa was picking out clothes too.

"I exercise." Mostly activities that didn't need special clothing or equipment.

"I know. I just can't picture you standing on your head." A drawer thumped shut.

"Can you picture Peter doing that?"

"Peter? No way." Vanessa hooted in disbelief.

"They're having a partner yoga class," Kate explained, "and he said he'd go. So, any suggestions on what I should wear?"

"How about stretchy pants and a T-shirt? You don't have any spandex exercise clothes, do you?"

"Not a stitch." Kate shuddered at the idea of wearing tight, brightly colored gym clothes. *So* not her style. Hunkering down, she dug around in her bottom drawer and found a lightweight pair of black lounging pants that would do.

"Was there anything else, Mom? Not to rush you, but I really need to go take a shower in a minute if I'm going to have time for breakfast."

Kate straightened, catching her breath before answering. "Yes, actually there is. What do you think about the idea of helping Paige with a vintage fashion show to benefit a women's shelter she works with? Maybe you and your roommates could model."

Vanessa gasped. "Mom, are you serious? That sounds fab. Maddie and Zoe are going to freak when I tell them about it."

"Hold off, OK? I want to run it by Bebe first. After all, we're going to borrow some of her clothes, maybe." It might be a good idea to round out the show with thrift shop finds.

Ideas for crazy outfits flashed into her head, and she started to feel excited. This could be really fun.

"I won't tell anyone, promise." She squealed again. "I'm so excited. Sorry, but I've really got to run. Talk to you later. Love you."

Kate smiled at her daughter's enthusiasm as she closed the suitcase and zipped it shut. Although she missed Vanessa living at home terribly, she had to admit that the new relationship they were forging as friends was really wonderful.

After setting her suitcase by the front door, she went to her studio to pack. In addition to her laptop, notebooks, and design reference books, she packed crochet supplies. Should she take the dressmaker's form? She often used it when working on larger garments, and it would be handy when Ariel wasn't around for fittings. After taking her box of supplies to the front door, she returned for the bulky mannequin. *That's why I drive a van, right?*

The doorbell rang as she set the form down, and a look through the peephole revealed Vivi. She gave the mannequin a smile when Kate opened the door. "I'd ask if you're all packed, but I see you're taking your whole workshop with you."

"Just about. I never know what I'll need so I tend to overpack." Kate stepped aside to let her friend enter.

Vivi gave the mannequin a friendly pat as she passed. "I think we'll need to take both cars to the farm. I won't be able to stay there full time until the retreat starts."

"Do you have time for a coffee? I'm ready for a second cup." Kate went to the kitchen and Vivi followed her.

"How was your date last night?" Vivi asked, sliding into a seat at the table.

Kate popped a mocha pod into the coffeemaker for Vivi. "It was great. Paige made a wonderful meal, and we had a good time with her and Patrick." There was no way she was going to share details about Peter's good-night kiss. Changing the subject quickly, she said, "Peter told me there's no news about Martha's whereabouts yet." She poured water into the machine and pushed the button. "After yesterday's events, I think Bebe might have been the intended victim."

"Because of Slim's offer and the threat?" Vivi pondered this idea. "You could be right. They do look kind of similar." Her face fell. "That means Bebe may be in danger. What if the assailant tries again?"

Kate set her friend's mug in front of her. "Exactly." As she made herself a cup, she filled Vivi in on her reasoning. "And I also have another theory. I think Martha might be an abused wife or girlfriend."

"My goodness, Kate." Vivi's eyes shone with admiration. "You could very well be right. Why else would she be using an assumed name and avoiding people? She's hiding from someone."

Kate sat down with her own mug. "She still might turn out to be a criminal on the run, but hearing about the women's shelter gave me a different slant on her actions." She took a sip of coffee. "If I'm right, I hope her abuser doesn't find her first."

Vivi bit her lip, her brow furrowed. "What can we do? I hate sitting back and doing nothing."

"I don't like it either. One thing I'd like to do today is call those employers on Martha's résumé to see if we can learn something. And I'd also like to go to the library and do some background research for both cases."

"Let me double-check my schedule." Vivi pulled out her phone. "I don't have anything until this afternoon. So, if you go right now, I'll be able to come with."

The grinding noise of a backhoe drifted in from outside. The workers were back, fortunately a little later than most mornings. Kate got up, took her cup to the sink, and rinsed it. "That's our cue to get out of here."

Vivi followed Kate's van in her Mini. They drove to the central library in Fort Worth, which was adorned with massive columns in the front like a government edifice or national monument. They easily found spaces in the parking garage and were soon inside.

"This place is like a museum," Vivi whispered as they entered the main room. She had to keep her voice low since every sound echoed in the high-ceilinged room. The interior continued the outside's grandeur with additional giant columns and huge paintings in gilded frames.

"That was my thought when I first came here too." Kate had visited this library to investigate other mysteries in which she'd found herself immersed. She hoped the library's excellent databases would once again help her find key clues. As she'd learned, they contained deeper and more complete information than could be found on the Internet.

At the reference desk, they obtained two-hour passes to use the system. Then they found computers in adjoining carrels and logged on.

"What do you want me to do?" Vivi asked.

"How about looking up contact information for the employers on Martha's résumé?" Kate handed her the manila folder. "The directories here are more complete than you can find online."

Vivi opened the folder, peered at the page, and began to tap keys. "What are you going to do?"

"I think I'll dig into Slim Baker and see what I can find out." Peter had mentioned a chain of convenience stores

Slim owned, so she looked first at general business news and then logged onto the corporate registration and deed transfer databases. After a few tries, she found the transfer of ownership of property from Baker Enterprises, Inc., to Worthy Stores, LLC.

Out of curiosity, she dug into the new owners of the Worthy Stores chain. She found only brief news items mentioning the sale, and the corporate website listed no information concerning ownership or management. She switched back to the county business database and saw the name of an attorney who served as their registered agent. She jotted down the name, Brendan Oliver.

Perhaps it meant nothing, but she'd learned to get details about every recent action a suspect made. That was how connections and motives were uncovered.

"Look at this." Vivi leaned back in her chair and gestured to Kate, her face eager.

"Did you find the employers?" Kate scooted her chair over so she could view Vivi's screen.

"Oh, a long time ago." She showed Kate the résumé, which was now marked in pen with phone numbers and names. "When I went to use the bathroom, I tried calling the second and third jobs. They never heard of her. Only the first one had. She was an executive assistant at Eagle Oil Products."

"And that's the only one Bebe called, I believe. Good work."

"So then I decided to search for recent domestic abuse cases in the Houston area." She stabbed the résumé with her finger. "Before the date on this last job here." She pointed at the screen. "Look."

"Woman found injured on sidewalk." The dateline was a small town just outside Houston. "Mary Benson, 53, was found sitting on the sidewalk outside her apartment house late Friday night by a neighbor. She was suffering from a black eye and a bloody nose and seemed 'dazed,' according to the person who found her. When questioned, Benson could give no information about her attacker, claiming to have been mugged. Police are questioning Sylvester Vink, the male companion Benson was seen with earlier that evening, to see if he can shed light on the events of that night."

"This is interesting, Vivi, and the dates fit. But without a picture, there's no way to know if that Mary Benson is actually Martha."

Vivi's fingers flew across the keyboard as she brought up another Web page. She stretched out her arms and shook her fingers, smiling smugly. "Voilà."

Kate stared at the Web page in amazement.

Nine

Kate gave a low whistle, earning the glare of an elderly man nearby. "That's amazing. How did you find that?" The woman with long blond hair depicted in a "selfie" photograph on a social network page dated a couple of years earlier definitely resembled the woman they knew as Martha.

"Simple. Once I had a name and town, I searched. Fortunately for us, she didn't delete her account."

"Print that. We need to give it to Peter. And the article."

"He can probably pull her driver's license and make sure Martha is really Mary." Vivi sent the pages to the printer. "Did you have anything else you wanted to look up?" She glanced at the wall clock. "I have a little more time."

Kate shared what she had learned about Slim Baker, which wasn't anything definitive. "While we're here, we might as well look up Derek Morehouse."

Vivi sent her a sharp look. "Why is that?"

"Mostly in the interest of leaving no stone unturned, I guess. Both Bebe and Ariel have implied that he has money problems. And where there are money problems—"

Vivi finished the sentence for her. "There could be murder. Say no more."

"I've got the corporate site up, so let's use my computer." Kate returned to her station, and Vivi edged over to sit next to her.

Derek's Fort Worth company, More Models, was registered

with the county. The registered agent was Brendan Oliver.

Kate's hackles rose. "That's the same lawyer Worthy Stores uses." She switched back to the other window. "See?"

Vivi shrugged. "It might be a coincidence. Maybe he specializes in business law."

"If I've learned one thing, it's that there are no coincidences."

"Now you really sound like a police officer." Vivi grinned. "Let's see what we can find out about Derek in general."

Kate did an Internet search and found articles going back decades about Derek's career as a fashion photographer. Some mentioned Bebe, and Kate sent them to the printer to read more closely later. Finally, a story from a Los Angeles newspaper dated two years earlier caught her eye.

"Storied Model Agency Falls on Hard Times." The article talked about the history and decline of Derek's California agency. Apparently, he had to file for bankruptcy.

"I'm guessing Bebe is helping him get back on his feet," Kate said. "Remember that comment she made about a loan she gave him?"

"Sure do. Very generous of her," Vivi said. "Not sure I'd do it, if I had an ex. Let's check out a couple more sites. Then I've really got to go."

Kate opened links to a Fort Worth newspaper's social page. "Uh-oh." She pointed at the screen. Ariel and Derek had been photographed standing with drinks at a charity event. Leaning in between them, arms around their shoulders, was Slim Baker. The three of them were beaming. "I wonder if Bebe knows how cozy her ex is with her enemy."

In the parking garage, Vivi roared off in her Mini with a promise to come to the farm later. Kate decided to call Peter before getting on the road herself. Poised to leave a message on his voice mail, she felt a rush of warm happiness when his deep voice said, "Hey."

She felt a smile stretch across her mouth. "Hey, yourself." In the background, she heard voices and ringing phones. Peter must have been at the station.

"Let me go somewhere quiet." She heard the sounds of footsteps and a door clanking open and shut. "I had a great time last night." By his echoing voice, she guessed he was in the stairwell.

"So did I." For a moment she basked in the pleasure of being connected to him, even if only by telephone. "But I didn't call about that. I found some new information about Martha Brown."

He sucked in his breath. "Really? How?"

"Actually, Vivi found it. She had the bright idea to search in the Houston area for domestic violence cases."

"Domestic violence?"

"I guess I thought of it because of Paige's shelter. I mentioned it to Vivi, and based on the résumé and the last job date, she searched in the Houston area. After she found a case, she used the name of the woman—Mary Benson—to find a social media profile. It's her."

"Wow. Great work. I'm really impressed."

"Thanks. She and I make a good team." Kate took a deep breath, hoping she was convincing him. "It all fits, Peter. That's why she was trying to live under a new name. And why she disappeared from the hospital. She didn't want her abuser to find her."

"And we posted her license all over the media, looking

for her." Peter's tone was grim. "Tell me what you have. We'll locate the perp before he finds her again."

A chill ran down Kate's spine. The publicity around her injury and disappearance might lead Mary's abuser right to her. "I've got hard copies of the news article and the social media page. I could bring them by." Then she had a bright idea. "I know. I'll take photos of them with my cellphone and email them to you. Will that work?"

"As long as they're clear. I'd take you out to lunch, but I'm going into a meeting with the chief in five minutes."

"That's all right. I'm going out to the farm now anyway. But I'll take a rain check."

They agreed to touch base later. After they hung up, Kate took photos of the documents and emailed them. Then she started the van and headed out of the garage toward the highway.

The trip to the farm felt familiar by now, and she made it in good time. Hers was the only vehicle in the visitor lot, and she parked closest to the barn where she would be staying. As she got out of the van, Bebe emerged from around the back of the house, wearing a wide-brimmed, white gardening hat and gloves with her usual uniform of jeans and T-shirt. She carried a flat basket holding cut flowers.

Waving a hand in greeting, she hurried over. "Good morning, Kate. I'm so happy you're going to be staying here." She beamed. "With you and Vivi and the retreat guests, I'll have a full house for the first time."

"Thanks for having me." Smiling in return, Kate opened the back of the van. "I hope everything goes well this weekend." She deeply and sincerely hoped there would be no more dangerous turn of events.

Bebe spotted the mannequin and laughed. "I see you brought a friend."

"I guess you can't accuse me of traveling light." Kate reached for her suitcase. "Where should I take this? Everything else will go in the wardrobe room."

"I've put you in a room upstairs." Still holding the basket of flowers, she led the way toward the barn. The original double barn doors were still in place, but Bebe opened a small side door into the main room. This had soaring beams and a wagon-wheel chandelier hanging from a thick chain. Two groups of sofas and chairs and a long dining table partially filled the space. Kate noticed there was plenty of room for yoga classes at one end, marked by a stack of exercise mats under a window. Drywall had been applied to the interior walls, and they were presently a dull white splotched with gray joint compound along the seams.

"You can see why this room needs to be painted." Bebe set the flowers on the dining table next to a vase. "Does your daughter want the job?" With a gesture, she walked toward a wide staircase along one wall.

"I spoke to her this morning, and yes, she's asking a group of friends to help. When do you want them?"

"When can they come?" Bebe laughed. "As soon as possible would be great." On the second floor, she showed Kate to a room with a view of the orchard. Although not large, it was furnished with a comfy-looking queen-size bed and an upholstered chair and ottoman in a traditional yet updated style. A dish of dried lavender added to the ambiance, and Kate pictured herself relaxing in the chair with a crochet project before crawling into that comfy bed. "This is really nice, Bebe." She placed the suitcase on a stand and went to the window to peer down into the gardens.

"I'm glad you like it. There are four rooms up here and four downstairs." She opened a door. "You'll be sharing this bathroom with the room next door, which is where I'll put Vivi."

"Perfect." The bathroom had a huge soaking tub and was stocked with salts and oils, all claiming to offer relaxation. Kate amended her plan to include a long hot bath before crocheting in the armchair. "I'll call Vanessa right away and see if they can come over today," she said as she followed Bebe downstairs.

"That would be wonderful." Bebe paused by the table and began to put the flowers into the vase. "The house is open if you want to take in your design supplies. I'll either be in here or the garden."

Kate unloaded the rest of her things from the van, including the dress form, and carried them into the wardrobe room she was using as a studio. Being able to refer to the clothing while she worked rather than photographs was an incredible opportunity. That thought gave her an idea, and she draped the mannequin with the beginnings of her next project, a knee-length dress with angel sleeves, and placed it next to the worktable.

After setting out her supplies, she called Vanessa and learned that she had rounded up a group of friends who could come that afternoon. Then she touched base with Vivi and asked her to pick up pizzas and soda in Magnolia Creek on her way after work. Bebe had already arranged for delivery of paint and supplies.

Before starting her next design, Kate took a few deep breaths and gazed out at the exuberant garden. It seemed like new flowers and bushes were blooming every time she came out here. Once she felt ready, her mind at peace, shoulders relaxed, she picked up her hook and thread and began to create.

"Where should we begin, Miz Stevens?" Gil, one of Vanessa's friends, pushed long bangs out of his eyes as he considered the high-ceilinged room complicated by French doors, the double barn door, windows, and a staircase. Gil, Jack, Ben, Maddie, Zoe, and Vanessa made up the team Vanessa had recruited for the job.

"My dad says you should always cut in around the edges first," Jack said. "Then you don't have to worry about staining the ceiling or floor with the paint roller."

"That sounds like a plan, Jack," Kate said. "Let's get everyone doing that, girls at floor level, guys on the stepladders. But first let's move the furniture into the middle of the room and put down drop cloths."

Vanessa plugged in a portable music player and speakers, and the group began to move furniture to the accompaniment of lively rock songs, laughter, and chatter. Kate and Vivi unplugged lamps and picked up ornamental items and stashed them in the small galley kitchen.

"I'll go get the pizzas from the car and bring them in here," Vivi said. "I've got them in those bags that keep them hot. I borrowed them from the hotel."

"Great." Kate opened the fridge, which was turned on but empty. "There's plenty of room for the soda."

Once the room was prepped, Kate and Vivi opened gallons of silvery-green paint and filled cans and roller trays. The kids worked fast and efficiently, and within a couple of hours, the painting was complete.

When Bebe came over to check on their progress, the boys were putting the furniture back into place while the girls washed the brushes in the utility room at the back of the barn. "What a great job," she said, gazing around in appreciation. Night had fallen so the hanging chandelier and the lamps were blazing, illuminating the transformed room. The French doors and windows stood open to air out the paint odor.

"We're getting ready to have pizza if you want to join us," Kate said.

"Two of them are veggie," Vivi said, guessing the model probably didn't like pepperoni.

"I'd like that, thanks. Let's go eat on the porch."

The group gathered there, the kids sitting on the steps. For a few minutes, the only sounds were the munching of pizza and gulping of soda. Tansy the hen pecked around their feet, searching for stray crumbs.

"Miss Morehouse," Zoe said, her dark eyes intense with hero worship, "it's so exciting to meet you."

"Yeah, we're all big fans," Maddie said, pointing to herself and her roommates.

"We are too," Ben said and received an elbow from Gil.

"Thank you, that's nice to hear," Bebe said. "But please, call me Bebe."

"How did you become a model?" Zoe asked.

Bebe took in the girl's long, slender limbs and pretty, fine-boned face. A smudge of paint still adorned her button nose. "Are you thinking about modeling?"

One of the boys whistled. "Hush!" Vanessa said. "I want to hear this."

Zoe ducked her head. "Kind of. People tell me I should."

Bebe gave a slight sigh, and Kate wondered if she experienced the same well-meant questions Kate did concerning writing. Both were attractive occupations, but people often didn't realize how much hard work and determination it took to succeed. Talent was only the beginning.

"The first step is to see if you're photogenic. The second is to ask yourself if you have the drive to succeed in the face of rejection, long hours, and often bad working conditions."

Kate bit back a smile. Except for the photogenic part, it sounded remarkably like getting started in a writing career.

"But you can make a lot of money, right?" Maddie asked. "Otherwise, who would do it?"

"You can. If you have the right look and are easy to work with." Bebe studied Zoe's face again. "You do have an interesting bone structure. I'd like to see some photos. Try to get some experience, even on an amateur level. Make sure you enjoy doing it."

Zoe squealed and gave Maddie, sitting next to her, a hug. "I'm so excited."

"I know how all of you can get some modeling experience," Kate said. "A local women's shelter is putting on a fashion show, if you're interested."

Now all three girls squealed. "Mom, we'd love to," Vanessa said. "What's the theme?"

"Vintage clothes." Kate nodded at Bebe. "Inspired by your collection." She'd decided to let the woman offer to lend them clothing rather than ask, considering the value of the designer pieces. If she didn't, they'd shop at vintage stores or borrow from friends and relatives.

To her delight, Bebe offered right away. "I have a few pieces you can use. More than a few, actually."

"That's wonderful, Bebe," Vivi said. "I'm sure they'll be a big draw."

"Actually, I'd love to help curate the show. I picked up a lot of fashion knowledge during my career."

"What a fantastic offer," Kate said. "My friend who's putting on the show, Paige Bryant, will be so excited. I think having you involved will really boost people's interest." She pictured advertising mentioning the model's name, maybe even featuring her picture.

"That's for sure," Vivi said. "It'll be a sold-out event."

"Glad to help," Bebe said. She ducked her head, her cheeks pinking. Kate realized that despite her fame, Bebe was actually a modest person who enjoyed helping others.

Vanessa turned to the men. "You can be in the show too."

"Yeah," Maddie said, "we'll need guys onstage with us."

Gil rolled his eyes. "Us? Model? You've got to be kidding."

"Yeah, who wants to look at your ugly mug?" Jack mock-punched Gil in the arm. Gil play-shoved him back. "Hey! You're no prize either."

Bebe pursed her lips and cocked her head, pretending to give them the once-over. "All of you are adequately handsome. I think we do need you for the show."

In response, the young women hooted and whistled, and with much laughter, the men agreed to model for the fashion show as long as they didn't have to wear makeup.

After cleaning up their plates and cans, the gang gratefully pocketed Bebe's generous cash payment, climbed into their cars with calls of thanks, and headed back to Regency College.

As the taillights disappeared down the driveway, Vivi stretched out both arms with a yawn. "What are you ladies going to do? I'm thinking about hitting that big bathtub with a book myself."

Kate considered. Although it had been a long day, she wasn't really tired yet. "I might do a little more design work. I made a good start on a dress today, and I'd like to keep going."

Bebe stood. "I'll be in my office upstairs if either of you

need anything." She made a face. "There are some bookkeeping chores I've put off too long."

"I know what you mean," Kate said. "That's one of the downsides of owning a business—doing the books."

Vivi, partway down the path, called back, "Better you than me. Good night!"

Inside the studio, lamplight cast a welcoming glow on the worktable and her preliminary design. Kate spent a few minutes studying the garment on the mannequin to get herself back into the groove. Not for the first time, she marveled at the infinite possibilities offered by a piece of string and a hook. The dress had a subtle paisley design that was period appropriate as well as appealing.

Kate picked up her pencil and began sketching. The trilling of tree frogs drifted through the open French doors, the only sound in the evening landscape. Soon night fell completely, and not even a sliver of moon illuminated the dark garden.

A golden beam of headlights from the main road touched the tops of the trees edging the property. They passed. A moment later, the lights moved back the other way. The third pass caught Kate's attention. This remote rural road surely didn't get much traffic at any time of day, let alone one car right after another. Maybe someone was lost.

Deciding she really couldn't do anything about it and certainly wasn't going to go out there to investigate, Kate bent over her work again. Then a rapping at the front door startled her. She waited for a moment to see if Bebe would come downstairs. When the knocking sounded a second time, she went out into the hallway.

Wondering what to do, she stared at the front door. She crept quietly across the creaky hardwood floor to the sidelights and peered out. The porch light wasn't turned on, so she couldn't see anything more than a tall, dark shape standing there.

Where was the light switch? She found a bank of switches along the wall and flicked each, finally touching the right one. When she peered out again, she saw a big man with long, greasy hair, hulking shoulders, and a handlebar mustache standing in front of the door. He swung his big head back and forth, rolled his shoulders, and lifted his hand to knock again.

"Who is it?" she called.

"Is Mary Benson there?" he called, his voice muffled by the thick door.

Shock jolted Kate. She realized with a sick certainty that Mary Benson's abuser was on the other side of the door. Her heart began to pound and her breath came in short bursts.

"There's no one here by that name," she called as loudly as possible.

Will he try to get in? Feeling as if she were moving in slow motion, she slid her hand to the deadbolt and turned it to the locked position. To her horror, the brass doorknob immediately began to violently twist back and forth.

Ten

Anger rose up in Kate, replacing the fear with a boost of adrenaline. "Mary is not here," she almost shouted. "You better leave before I call the police."

The knob turned a few more times.

"I'm dialing them right now." Kate hit Peter's speed dial number.

Footsteps thumped on the porch, and she heard the sound of a vehicle spraying gravel.

She was leaving Peter a voice mail when Bebe came running down the stairs. "What's going on, Kate? I thought I heard you yell."

"Please call me as soon as you get this." She disconnected. "I did yell. We had an intruder. He tried to get into the house, so I said I was calling the police." She waved the phone. "Which I did."

Bebe sank down onto a step. Her face was white with fear. "What do you mean?"

"Today Vivi and I did some research and learned Martha's real identity. She is an abused woman named Mary Benson." Kate flipped through her phone to the documents she'd sent to Peter and handed the phone to Bebe. "Take a look."

"You weren't kidding when you said you investigate mysteries." She squinted at the document, moving the phone close, then away. "Darn. I need my reading glasses." She glanced around and spotted a pair on a small table, got up, and put them on. After studying the information for a couple of minutes, she looked up. "Now we know why she was using a fake name. She's been running for her life." She handed the phone back to Kate.

Clasping the phone, Kate sat on a ladder-back chair that rested against one wall. "That's what I think too. Unfortunately, when the police put the word out that she was missing from the hospital, it informed her abuser that she was in the area."

Bebe tapped her lips with one finger. "But didn't he already know? He attacked her right here at the farm."

Kate's thoughts raced. Should she tell Bebe that she might have been the intended victim, not Mary? She'd been hoping that Peter would be the one to share the news that she could be in danger.

Deciding it wasn't a good idea to wait, she took a deep breath. "That could be true, and since he knows she's missing, he's come back here. Or," Kate said, trying to think how to put it delicately, "the attack might have been intended for you."

Bebe's mouth dropped open. "Me? Why would someone want to hurt *me*?"

"You just received a threat in the mail," Kate reminded her gently. "Someone's upset with you."

She shook her head with a grimace. "Over a land dispute? That seems like excessive use of force."

Kate knew from her experience that motivation for murder and other criminal acts often seemed flimsy to law-abiding people. "There's a lot of money at stake, right? That often brings out the worst in people."

Bebe nodded. "That's true. But the person hit Martha—I mean Mary—right on the head. Surely he must have seen her face first."

"You're similar in looks, close in age, and you both have long blond hair." She snapped her fingers. "Maybe he doesn't know either of you. That would explain him attacking the wrong person."

Kate's phone rang in her hand, making her jump. It was Peter. She snatched it up and answered. "Peter, I'm so glad you got back to me right away. I think Mary's abuser was just here. Sylvester Vink."

"Are you all right?" At her reassurance that everyone was fine, his tone became all business. "Take it from the top and tell me everything you remember."

She recounted the series of events, including the slow-moving car, the knocking on the door, and the intruder's attempt to get inside the house.

"Did you happen to get a look at his vehicle?"

"No, darn it. But he was quite distinctive in appearance." She relayed the man's physical description. "Do you think it's him?"

"Hold on. Let me check the system and see if he's in there." Peter clicked on his keyboard for a moment. "OK. Sylvester Vink, height six foot one, two hundred and fifty pounds. The photo shows long hair and a mustache." He whistled. "The dude's got quite a rap sheet."

"That sounds like the man I saw." Kate's heart sped up. His confirmation of her fears made her realize afresh what a close call they had experienced. What if he'd been able to get into the house? What would he have done to them?

"Kate, I'm going to put out an all-points bulletin on him. Please, lock up the house and stay put. Hopefully we'll pick him up before too long." He was silent for a moment. "Actually, I'm going to have the sheriff post a deputy out there for the night. I hate to think of you ladies being vulnerable if that creep comes back."

"Would you? I'd sleep better if you did." She glanced at

Bebe, who looked petrified. "I think we all would."

Bebe insisted on brewing calming cups of chamomile tea. After forcing herself to drink the grassy-tasting brew, Kate helped her go around the house and make sure that all the doors and windows were shut and locked. "Now let's go out and check the barn," Bebe said. She grabbed a flashlight and led the way across the yard.

Kate stopped short, struck by a horrible thought. *What if he's hurt Vivi?* Why on earth hadn't she gone to the barn to check? She began to run. "Vivi!" she cried out as she passed the other woman. Bebe caught on and began to trot behind her. They burst into the barn. A lamp burned on a table by the door, and in the upstairs hall, a night-light shone. All was quiet, serene, and seemingly undisturbed.

Kate pounded upstairs to Vivi's room and paused at the door, listening. Vivi must have gone to bed already. "Vivi?" she called. No answer.

"Do you think you should go in?" Bebe whispered.

"I hate to. But yes, I do." She turned the knob and pushed the door open, the light from the hallway revealing Vivi, lying on her side in one of the double beds. "I'll go check on her." She padded to the bedside and peered down at her friend, holding her breath until the gentle movement of the covers informed her that Vivi was still breathing. She turned to Bebe and gave her a grin and a thumbs-up.

As she backed away, Vivi grunted and flipped over onto her back. Her eyes flew open. Spotting Kate, she screamed.

Kate backed away. "Vivi, Vivi. It's me, Kate."

Vivi stopped screaming. "I'm sorry. You scared the life out of me." She patted her chest. "My heart is pounding so hard." She looked at Bebe standing in the doorway. "What's going on?"

"We had an intruder at the house," Kate said. "We were checking on you to make sure he didn't come out here."

"An intruder?" Vivi's eyes widened. "I bet it has to do with Mary Benson."

"Bingo. The police are coming over to watch the house so we'll be OK." She glanced over her shoulder at Bebe. "The outside doors lock, right?"

"Of course," Bebe said. "I'll show you. Then you two can get some rest."

With a groan, Vivi flopped back down onto the bed and pulled the sheet up over her face. "Good luck with that one."

"I hear you," Kate said. She doubted she'd sleep a wink herself. She followed Bebe downstairs to make sure the French doors and back door were locked. After Bebe left, Kate watched to be sure she made it back to the house safely before shutting and bolting the door. Then she made another circuit of the doors and windows to double-check they were secure. Finally satisfied that the barn was secure, she went upstairs to get ready for bed. First she peeked into Vivi's room. She smiled when she heard the sound of soft snoring.

After undressing and washing up, Kate got into bed, enjoying the feel of the silky sheets and warm blankets. She lay still for a few minutes, staring at the ceiling. It was no use. Her thoughts scrambled in circles like a squirrel in a cage. She sat up and flung back the covers. Only one thing would help. Crochet.

Reaching into her tote, Kate pulled out the pattern and soft yarn she was going to use as the class project at the retreat. She always tested a pattern before teaching it to ensure it was appropriate for her students. Some so-called beginner patterns were anything but easy.

She plopped into the wide, upholstered armchair and

began to crochet, the repetitive movements providing the relaxation she craved. She had almost completed the sample headband when her head began to bob. The third time her chin touched her chest, she put the project aside and crawled into bed.

Ah. There was nothing like crochet. She believed that handwork rivaled sleeping pills, meditation, and yoga for promoting restful sleep. It was certainly better than the herbal tea Bebe had given her earlier.

She fell quickly into a deep sleep.

Hours later, she jerked awake. Was it a sound that had disturbed her? Something unusual in the quiet country night? She strained her eyes and ears, using every faculty to penetrate the pitch-black of the room.

A floorboard creaked. Kate focused her eyes on the dark rectangle of the doorway. A tall, hulking shadow moved. It detached itself from the doorway and approached the bed.

Someone is in my room!

Eleven

She blinked, at first not certain if she was still asleep and dreaming. Then the figure shifted and lurched forward. Kate sat bolt upright. "Vivi? Is that you?" she asked, although something told her it wasn't her friend. The person was much larger and wider for one thing. And surely Vivi would have said something rather than creeping in silently.

In response, the figure turned on a flashlight and shone it right in her face. "Hey!" she protested, flinging up an arm to block the harsh beam. Her heart began to pound. It definitely wasn't Vivi or even Bebe. Had Sylvester Vink come back and broken into the building? Panic flooded her body. She opened her mouth and screamed at the top of her lungs.

In the room next door, she heard banging around as Vivi woke up and came to see what was wrong. Kate screamed again, and the figure turned and ran out of the room. She heard the loud thumps of footsteps on the stairs. Vivi burst into the room. "Kate? What's wrong? Are you all right?"

"No." Kate reached over and switched on the bedside lamp. "Someone broke in. He shined a flashlight right into my face."

Vivi gasped, one hand going to her mouth. "Are you serious? How did he get in?"

Kate threw back the covers and swung her legs out of bed. "I don't know. Let's go check." The whole situation was a woman's worst nightmare come true, a stranger in her bedroom at night. Now that Vivi was with her, the adrenaline began to seep away and her entire body felt shaky.

Vivi cast a fearful glance at the door. "What if he's still in the house?"

"I don't think so. I heard him run downstairs." She cocked her head, listening. "He's probably gone by now."

"Still." Vivi went to the bedroom door and locked it. Then she plopped down on the end of the bed, making the mattress bounce. "I'd feel a lot safer if we just call Peter."

"You're probably right." Kate's phone sat on the bedside table, and she picked it up and hit the speed dial for Peter.

Despite the late hour, he answered immediately. "Kate."

At the sound of his deep, warm, concerned voice, fear and horror washed over her again and she started to tremble. She opened her mouth to reply, but nothing came out. Instead, tears began to gush and silent sobs wracked her body.

"Kate?" Peter said again, his tone sharpening when she didn't answer.

Vivi took the phone from Kate's unresisting hand and quickly explained the situation to him. Peter punctuated her story with choice words regarding the competence of Magnolia Creek's deputy sheriff.

"Is Kate all right?" he barked.

"Yes, just scared," Vivi said. She pulled the phone away. "He didn't touch you, did he, Kate?"

She shook her head, kneading her hands together. What if she had been alone? What would he have done to her? She heard Peter talking, and then Vivi disconnected.

"He'll be right out. And he wants us to wait up here." Vivi went to the bathroom door. "I'm going to get dressed. And lock my own room." She went through the connecting door to her bedroom.

Kate sat for a moment, still attempting to absorb what had happened. Somehow Vink had gotten past the deputy outside and had broken into the retreat center, even though the doors and windows had all been locked. That wasn't very comforting. After a few minutes of staring into space, her mind whirling with unanswered questions, she got up and put her jeans and T-shirt back on. She really didn't want Peter or anyone else to see her oversized nightshirt and faded boxers.

Fully dressed, Vivi came back into the room. "Oh, good. You're dressed." She plopped down on the bed again and bounced. "I have a feeling I'm not going to get any sleep tonight." She looked surprisingly perky for someone who had been awakened in the middle of the night—twice. "What are we going to do while we wait?"

"I don't know about you," Kate said, "but I'm too wound up to sit and do nothing." Her gaze fell on the crochet project. "Want to make a headband?" She set Vivi up with a hook and yarn and gave her instructions. Then she called the house to check on Bebe.

She answered immediately. "Kate. Is everything all right?"

Kate sighed. "Not exactly." She gave Bebe the news of Vink's reappearance and told her to stay in the house. Help was on the way.

Peter called Kate when he arrived. "He's downstairs," Kate told Vivi after she hung up. "He didn't want to knock because he figured we wouldn't answer."

Vivi launched herself out of the armchair. "Good thinking."

Her heart singing with relief, Kate ran downstairs, still clutching her phone, with Vivi on her heels. If it hadn't been for the blue lights washing along the ceiling, she would have called him again to double-check that he really was standing outside the door. She unclicked the locks and opened the door, thinking as she did so that the intruder must have gotten in another way.

Peter stood on the step, his rumpled hair and wrinkled

shirt indicating he had rolled out of bed and dressed hastily. When his eyes settled on Kate's face, their worried expression touched something deep inside her. Without thinking, she launched herself into his arms. "Oh, Peter. I'm so glad to see you."

He clasped her tightly and lifted her off the floor for a good long squeeze. Then he set her down again. "I'm just glad that you and Vivi are all right."

When he turned, Kate noticed the uniformed officer standing behind him. "What happened, Deputy Webb?"

Webb's face was grim. "I'm sorry, ladies. I was parked at the foot of the driveway most of the night, but then I got called away for an emergency. He must have sneaked back onto the property then." He shook his head. "He certainly didn't get past me."

"A case of bad timing then," Peter said. "Why don't you go to the house and check on Ms. Morehouse while I find out how he got in?"

Before Webb made it to the house, Bebe came trotting down the path in slippers, a white silk bathrobe billowing behind her. "I saw the blue lights so I figured it was safe to come outside." She looked both shocked and scared. "Is everyone all right?"

"We're fine," Kate said.

"I'm so glad." Her shoulders slumped in relief as she turned to Peter. "Hello again, Detective Matthews."

"Please, call me Peter." He gestured toward the retreat center door. "Let's go find out what happened."

Kate and Vivi moved aside, allowing Peter and Deputy Webb to enter. Kate, Vivi, and Bebe followed them as they made a circuit of the downstairs, checking windows and doors. At the rear of the building, they found the breach. A pane of glass had been broken, and the intruder had reached in and unlocked the back door.

"He must have left this way too." Vivi pointed to the door, which was still slightly ajar.

"Sure looks like it." Peter glanced at Bebe. "I recommend getting an alarm system. This door is far enough away from the upstairs rooms that no one heard him break the glass."

"I guess I'd better. I can't take the chance of putting my guests at risk." Bebe frowned. "You'd think we'd be safe so far out in the country."

Deputy Webb nodded his head sagely. "That's why a lot of crime happens in the country, ma'am. Some folks out here don't even lock their doors, and criminals know that."

Bebe appeared ready to chew him out, so Kate stepped in. "Actually, in this case, we were specifically targeted. He seems to think Mary Benson is still here."

"Maybe we should put up a sign," Vivi said flippantly. "This was the second try tonight."

"We need to find both of them before someone else gets hurt." Using a gloved hand, Peter pulled the door open and stepped out onto the stone step. He gestured to the deputy. "Bring your flashlight out here. Let's see if he left anything behind." The other man complied, pulling a long, heavy flashlight out of his belt as he trotted through the doorway.

While the women watched, the men crisscrossed the area behind the retreat center, the beams from their flashlights scanning back and forth across the ground. "What are they looking for?" Bebe asked.

"Footprints, anything he dropped, something they can tie back to the intruder, Sylvester Vink," Kate said.

"Sylvester Vink?"

Kate explained what she and Vivi had learned at the library.

"That's impressive." Bebe's voice was full of admiration. "You two really are good investigators. The police are lucky to have your help."

Vivi grinned at this praise, but Kate said quickly, "Peter's really good at his job. He would have figured it out sooner or later. We just came across some of the information first." She blushed at her prompt and vigorous defense of Peter.

Fortunately, Peter's shout distracted everyone. Disregarding protocol, they hurried to see what he had found. In the steady beam of the flashlight, they clearly saw he was holding a piece of black cloth. "This was snagged on a rosebush," Peter said. "Was the intruder wearing black, Kate?"

She thought for a moment, casting her memory back to the hulking figure looming in her room. "I couldn't see his clothing clearly since it was dark in my room." Then a memory flashed into her mind. She visualized the bouncing light from his own flashlight as he turned and bolted. She'd gotten a quick glimpse of his sleeve. "Yes, he was. A black shirt. So was Vink earlier tonight."

Peter slipped the fabric into an evidence pouch. "This looks like it might have come from his shirt."

Despite a thorough search, the men didn't find anything else in the yard or the house. The deputy returned to his station on the road, while Peter entered the barn to find the women in the main room, where they were drinking tea Bebe had prepared in the small kitchen. Kate noted to her disappointment that it was chamomile again. She sincerely hoped it would help her relax as advertised since the taste was still not her cup of tea.

"Would you like some?" Bebe asked Peter.

He took a seat on the sofa beside Kate. "Sure. Thanks." He leaned back and ran a hand through his hair with a sigh. "What a long night."

"You need a statement from me, don't you?" Kate asked. She handed him the mug Bebe had poured from the teapot.

He sipped the tea, quickly hiding a grimace, to Kate's amusement. "I should. It's important to get them while the incident is fresh."

Kate shuddered at the memory of waking up to find Vink in her room. "I'll never forget it. It was horrible."

Distress flashed over Bebe's face. "Are you going to be able to sleep? I'll have an alarm put in tomorrow. I don't care what it costs."

"I'm staying right here tonight," Peter said, patting the sofa. "Obviously, locks don't keep that guy out. I'm not taking the chance of him coming back for a third time."

"I have extra bedrooms out here," Bebe said, "so you don't need to stay on the sofa."

"What a great idea," Vivi said. "I know I'll sleep better if you're here, Peter."

"Are you sure you don't mind?" Kate asked him. "Wouldn't you rather be at home?"

He smiled warmly at her. "Your safety is more important to me." He glanced at the others. "Yours too. Besides, I always carry a grooming kit and extra clothes in my truck, so I'm all set." He put his full mug down and stood. "I'll go get the statement forms and my bags."

At eight o'clock the next morning, Kate woke, surprised at how refreshed she felt despite the disturbances of the night. How much her restful sleep had to do with Peter's reassuring presence downstairs, she could only guess.

A soft knock came on the adjoining door, and then Vivi

poked her head in. "Good morning." She held two mugs and thrust one toward Kate. "Want this?"

Kate pushed herself to a sitting position. "As long as it isn't more of that herbal tea."

Vivi opened the door fully with her hip and entered. "Nope. Fresh-ground java, according to Bebe." After setting Kate's mug on the nightstand, she sat in the armchair and sipped her beverage.

"Is Peter still here?" Even saying his name made Kate's heart race a little faster. Either that or the coffee was really strong.

"I didn't see him, so I'm not sure." Vivi took another sip. "Tell you what, I slept a lot better with him here. I didn't even have a bad dream about some goon breaking in." She sipped again. "Gosh, I hope they find that guy. Today, preferably."

"Me too. And I hope they find Mary before he does." An idea sparked. "What are you doing today?"

Vivi gestured at her outfit of skirt, blouse, and sling-back shoes. "I have to run to the hotel, and then I'm all yours for the weekend."

"I'm going to go to Once Upon a Yarn for supplies and to talk to Paige. I think she might be able to help us."

Kate swung into the parking lot just as Paige was unlocking the front door of Once Upon a Yarn. There were plenty of open spaces this early in the day, and she was able to park right in front. She made sure her list was in the tote, climbed out, and went into the store.

Paige glanced up from the cash register. "Good morning, Kate. What brings you by so early?"

Kate dug out her list and set it on the counter. "I've got a busy day planned and thought I'd start with picking up some supplies." She smiled. "And pick your brain as well."

Paige laughed. "There isn't much to pick this hour of the day. I've barely had enough caffeine to function." She gestured toward the coffee station before going back to counting the money in the drawer. "Coffee is brewing if you want a cup."

"Thanks. I'll take one." She picked up the list. "But first I'll do my shopping and let you finish getting ready." She chose additional cones of white and ivory thread for the vintage garments and a colorful selection of yarns for the headband project. It would be fun to give the students their choice of colors. A multipack of colored hooks completed her selection.

Paige rang up the sale. Then they both sat with steaming cups of coffee in the attractive seating area near the front. Paige tapped a packet of sugar and ripped it open. "How's that handsome detective of yours?"

Kate smiled, knowing what she was about to say would startle her friend. "He had to spend the night last night."

Paige gasped in surprise, one hand to her mouth.

Kate laughed. "It's not what you think. You know me better than that. I just couldn't resist." She went on to explain the sequence of events at the farm and Peter's decision to play watchman.

Paige stirred her coffee again, vigorously. "It's a good thing he did. The whole thing sounds terrifying." She shook her head as she picked up her cup. "So, Bebe is going to install an alarm today?"

"Yes. She was on the phone with the company when I left after breakfast." Kate pondered how to bring up the next subject. She decided a direct approach was best. "Paige, can you tell me if Martha Brown, whose real name is Mary Benson, is staying at the shelter?"

"Why do you ask?" Paige fiddled with the sugar packets, giving Kate the feeling that she was avoiding an answer.

"I think she might be there. We learned that she was on the run from a man suspected of abusing her, and no one has been able to find her. It makes sense."

Paige looked up and met Kate's eyes. "I wish I could tell you." Her voice was passionate. "But we're bound to strict confidentiality rules. Your experience last night is evidence that many abusers just don't give up."

Kate felt a thrill of sympathetic fear for the plight of abused women. What she had gone through the previous night was bad enough, and she wasn't even the target. How terrible to live like a hunted animal. "I understand, Paige. I wouldn't want you to do anything you shouldn't. But if she *is* there, perhaps she could let the police know that she's safe."

Paige dropped her eyes again, this time ostensibly to arrange her spoon perfectly on a napkin. "Maybe she will."

"I have some good news," Kate said, changing the subject. "Bebe is going to let us use some of her vintage clothes for the fashion show. And Vanessa and her friends are going to model."

"That's fantastic. It's going to be a fabulous event." Paige reached for a pad of paper and a pen that were sitting on the coffee table. "Tell me more, and I'll take notes."

A productive hour later, Kate left Once Upon a Yarn to drive back out to the farm. She and Paige had made substantial progress brainstorming the fashions and format for the show. Her task was to talk to Bebe and identify the clothing she was willing to lend. Then she and Paige would choose additional outfits to round out the show, including the garments she was designing. Paige said she was going to dig into some boxes she and Patrick had stored in their attic, and Kate was going to ask Vivi if her mother had some things.

Even though Paige hadn't given her a firm answer, Kate fervently hoped that Mary was indeed at the shelter and would call the police. That would put her mind at ease about her safety, as would the arrest of Sylvester Vink.

With a sigh of aggravation, Kate pulled to a stop at yet another traffic light on the strip leading to the highway. She was getting all the red lights today. Across the intersection, an orange VW caught her eye. Could that be Phoebe Newland, the fired employee who had almost run them off the road? As the vehicle made a left in front of her and passed by, Kate saw it was indeed the young woman. She'd recognize that dark, spiky hair anywhere.

She watched Phoebe signal and pull into a gas station, driving over the curb on the way. She really *was* a bad driver. Kate glanced at the station's name: Worthy Gas & Go. And wasn't Worthy the name of the chain Slim Baker had owned?

On a hunch, Kate put on her blinker and turned right to follow.

Twelve

Instead of stopping under one of the pump canopies, Phoebe parked in the small lot. She hopped out and quickly strode inside, not seeming to notice Kate's van as she pulled up beside the VW. Kate grabbed her purse and followed, making sure to lock the van. The gas station and the surrounding businesses had the grimy, rundown appearance common to industrial fringe areas. *I wouldn't want to be out here at night*, she thought.

As Kate entered the store, the bored-looking, long-haired clerk glanced up briefly before returning to the newspaper he was reading. His tattooed arm rested on the counter while he made notes in pen with the other hand. Kate glanced around for Phoebe, but no one else was in the small space crammed with aisles of shelving and hemmed by beer and soda coolers. She spotted a coffee station at the rear and edged her way back there.

She picked up a coffee carafe off the burner and sniffed. *Ugh.* The smell of burnt coffee always turned her stomach. She didn't want to drink any more anyway, but buying a cup gave her an excuse to linger for a few minutes. *Where is Phoebe?* Maybe she was in the corner restroom, which was marked by a unisex sign. She slowly selected a small paper cup from the range of sizes on the counter and filled it with thick brew. Sugar and cream were next. She stirred with a wooden stick and pressed on a lid.

A burly man wearing a grimy T-shirt and a ball cap entered

the station and headed Kate's way. Instead of stopping for coffee, he opened the restroom door and went in. That answered the question of whether Phoebe was in there.

Unable to stall any longer, she made her way back to the cash register, wondering if she should buy a snack to tide her over until lunch. Breakfast had been hours ago. She glanced over the shelves and noticed something odd. While superficially they appeared full, closer examination showed that there were only a couple of each type of product and most of them were low-cost items. How could the store survive if it didn't have much to sell?

She grabbed a package of coffee cakes and went to the register. The clerk reluctantly moved his paper aside so she could set down her cup and package. "Anything else I can get you?" he asked in a monotone.

"No thanks." She reached into her purse for her wallet. A white swinging door at the rear burst open, and she glanced over to see if Phoebe was emerging. Instead, a tall man in a cowboy hat brushed past Kate with a surly frown, one huge boot almost connecting with her ankle. She pressed closer to the counter to avoid him.

"See ya," the cowboy said to the clerk, settling his hat more firmly on his head as he charged out of the store.

"Later," the clerk called. Then he told Kate the amount she owed. As he was sliding her bills into the register, she spotted an interesting wooden coin sitting in the penny dish. She picked it up and saw that it was embossed on both sides with an eagle carrying wheat, much like the one on the back of paper dollar bills.

"What's this?" she asked. "Toy money?"

The clerk's glare landed on the wooden coin, and he held out his hand for it. "That's mine. Give it." He threw it into the register and proceeded to count out her change. She tucked the change into her bag and picked up her purchases. Before she had reached the door, he was bent over his paper again.

Outside, Kate climbed into the van to wait. She set her coffee in the cup holder with no plans to actually drink it. Instead she found a bottle of water and opened her coffee cakes. Maybe Phoebe was in the back room. She couldn't imagine what was back there except offices or a kitchen, although the store didn't offer homemade food. Maybe she was applying for a job. Working in a dump like that would be quite a comedown after a position as Bebe's assistant.

After an hour, the cakes long gone and her stomach reminding her that lunch was required, she gave up. Phoebe was obviously going to stay there awhile. Kate started the van and backed out carefully, stopping with a jolt of the brakes when a gold Lexus zoomed into the lot. The car continued past the lot and stopped in a space at the front of the store. Kate had backed up fully when she saw the driver's door open.

Derek Morehouse climbed out. *Small world*, Kate thought. He turned to click the lock from his key fob and then disappeared inside. As Kate pulled out of the parking lot, she couldn't imagine what had brought Derek to that particular gas station. It certainly wasn't for the coffee. *Is he meeting Phoebe? If so, why?*

Kate stopped at a Magnolia Creek deli for sliced cheeses and meats, a loaf of homemade bread, and three-bean salad for lunch, thinking it wasn't fair to expect her hostess to provide all the meals. At the farm, she found a note from Bebe pinned to the front door. "Kate, I'm out in the greenhouse if you need me." She took the food and her supplies inside and unpacked them, then headed out to say hello.

It was another lovely spring day, and Kate enjoyed seeing the new flowers popping out on bushes and in the flower beds along the paths. On an impulse, she stopped and took a photo of clustered white and yellow daffodils and sent it via cellphone to her good friend Alice, who lived in Maine. "Want a taste of spring?" she wrote in the text. "Come visit!" Alice had been in Texas around Christmastime, and it would be wonderful to see her and her new husband, Jim, again.

Tansy came into view, busily pecking at the lush grass for worms. Kate greeted the chicken, feeling only slightly foolish, and felt flattered when the hen followed her along the path the way she did her owner. Kate had obviously been accepted into the hen's inner circle.

The greenhouses were large, rectangular structures where Bebe grew vegetables and flowers from seeds and cuttings. On such a warm day, she had left the door ajar and opened most of the upper windows. As Kate approached, one of the big automatic fans came on. Keeping the greenhouse at the right temperature meant cooling as well as heating, Bebe had explained on their tour of the grounds.

Kate stepped inside and savored the warm, moist air and the scent of green, growing things. Sometimes she thought she could live inside a greenhouse. Bebe was at the far end, watering vegetables growing in small black pots. Once the danger of frost was past, she'd transplant them into the garden.

The older woman looked up and smiled as Kate made her way through the tables covered with plants. "Hey, Kate. I was just thinking about lunch."

Kate's belly rumbled as if on cue. "I stopped and got sandwich fixings and bean salad."

Bebe set down her watering can and plucked a yellow leaf off a tomato plant. "You didn't have to do that. But thanks."

The fan unit in the rafters overhead came on, but in addition to the usual whir of blades, it began to make a strange rattling sound. Kate watched in horror as the huge metal object began to fall.

Thirteen

Acting on sheer instinct, Kate threw herself forward and knocked Bebe out of the way of the plummeting object, which came so close that she felt air gusting as it whizzed by. With a resounding crash, the fan landed on the table and smashed it flat, plants and dirt flying everywhere.

"Darn. Those plants were doing so well." Bebe's tone was deadpan. She caught Kate's eye and they both began to laugh.

"Thanks for saving my life," Bebe gasped as she wiped away tears. She kicked at a crushed plastic pot. "I would have been as flat as that."

Kate had a terrible thought. "Have you seen Tansy?"

Bebe glanced around. "No. Have you?"

"She followed me in here, I think." Kate felt sick. Then she heard a fierce clucking. The hen flew up and landed on top of the fallen fan, flapping her wings in disapproval. "Whew. I'm sure glad you're OK, Tansy."

"Me too." Bebe cooed at the chicken and stroked her feathers gently.

Kate moved back and tipped her head to study the brackets attached to the ceiling. Now that the shock was ebbing, she had enough presence of mind to question what had happened. The metal pieces up there looked intact, so she examined the fan. Nothing was broken, and she could clearly see where bolts were supposed to attach the housing to the rafters. She bent down and searched the floor. *Aha.* She found the object she was looking for and held it up.

"What is it?" Bebe's expression was one of puzzlement.

"It's a bolt. The fan didn't just fall. It was sabotaged."

"Sabotage? But who ... and why?" Bebe sagged back against a table, hands over her face. "This has nothing to do with Mary, does it?"

"I don't think so," Kate said gently. "Why would Sylvester Vink try to hurt you?"

"He wouldn't. But that begs the question, who would?" Her laugh was bitter. "Or I should ask, who would want to kill me? If it hadn't been for you ..." Her expression grew grim and determined. "I'm not going to just sit back and wait for the next 'accident.' We need to find out who did this."

"I agree." Kate patted her pocket. No phone. "I'll call Peter to report the incident in a minute, but let's take a look around first." Kate went to the rear door located next to where the fan had been attached; it was the logical entry for the saboteur. The greenhouse backed up to a wooded area, and Kate could plainly see a rudimentary path through the slender trees and underbrush.

First she examined the area around the door. Then, careful not to trample any evidence, she stepped into the woods, Bebe at her heels. The path was dry and there were no footprints in the dirt, no pieces of litter or scraps of cloth. If only people would conveniently leave traces as they passed by, like the piece of sweatshirt Vink had lost last night.

As the trees began to thin, Kate asked, "Where does this go?"

"See that stream?" Kate followed Bebe's pointing finger to the glitter of water in a ditch a short distance away. "That's the boundary line of my property."

"Who owns the other side?" Kate had a feeling she knew the answer.

"Slim Baker, now. It used to be ours."

The woods became a field, which extended to the ditch and continued on the other side. Slim's property was defined by a wire cattle fence. Whoever had come this way had to either climb or follow that fence. She found nothing in the long grass, but the bent blades showed the path someone had taken. In the soft mud bordering the stream, she finally had some luck.

Several large boot prints marked the spot where someone had jumped the stream. Then she realized something alarming. All the toes were pointed toward her.

The man was still on Bebe's property.

She whirled around and grabbed Bebe's arm. "Let's go. The intruder is still here somewhere."

Bebe's face went white. "What do you mean?"

Kate pointed at the prints and saw understanding dawn on the other woman's face. "What's the quickest route to the house? I left my phone there."

"I have an extension in the greenhouse. We can call from there."

With Kate in the lead, they scrambled up the bank. She ran as fast as she could, heart pounding, and the awareness that they could run into the prowler at any time stealing her air. She burst through the greenhouse door with relief and sagged against the nearest table. "Where's the phone?" she gasped.

Bebe pointed, just as winded as she was. Kate grabbed the receiver off the hook and entered Peter's number, which she had memorized. The thought flashed through her mind that it was unfortunate when you called the man you were dating to report a crime more often than to extend an invitation.

Peter picked up, and she quickly gave him the outline of what had happened. "Do you have any idea where the intruder is now?" he asked, his voice tense.

"No. He's not in the greenhouse, that's all I know."

"Hang on." He muffled the receiver for a moment and then came back on. "County is sending someone. I'll be right there. Ask Bebe if any doors lock out there."

She repeated the question, and Bebe nodded. "The storeroom locks." She pointed to a door in the back wall.

Peter had overheard. "Stay in there until the deputy shows up."

"Will do. Peter? Please hurry." Kate disconnected, then she and Bebe went into the storeroom, which had shelving around three sides filled with pots and trays and tools. From the strong smell of manure, Kate guessed the sacks stacked on the floor held fertilizer, probably organic to suit Bebe's values but smelly all the same. Bebe closed the door and locked it. It only had a button lock, but that would have to do.

"Gosh, I hope we don't suffocate before they get here," Kate said as the smell became stronger in the tight space.

"I hear you." Bebe flicked a switch and a small exhaust fan in the wall came on. "This should help."

Kate's natural reaction to stress was to pace, but the tiny area only allowed her to take three or four steps across, then back. In contrast, Bebe sat cross-legged on the floor and appeared to be meditating. Kate laughed. "I can clearly see the difference in our personalities."

Bebe's eyes popped open. Noting Kate's restless strides, she smiled. "Whatever works." A shudder ran down her erect spine. "I have to admit, it's a little harder than usual to stay calm. These incidents keep happening. And just last week I was thinking how bored I was."

"Boring sounds good about now." Kate took a step and pivoted. "But from my experience, it means we're coming to the end of this case. Actually, *cases*, plural. Everything goes haywire first."

"Maybe that's why Peter likes being a detective. All the adrenaline."

Kate stopped mid-stride. "I never thought of that. You could be right." And here she was, a peaceful little crochet designer, up to her neck in mysteries.

A knock sounded on the door. "Miss Morehouse? It's the police."

Bebe stood with a graceful leap and went to the door. "Show me your badge." She winked at Kate. "Under the door."

After some grunts and rustling, the badge came sliding under the door. Bebe picked it up, studied it, and handed it to Kate. She recognized Deputy Webb from the previous night.

Bebe unlocked the door and flung it open. "We've got to stop meeting like this." Her posture was elegant and commanding.

A red tide suffused the officer's neck and rose up into his young, clean-shaven cheeks. "Yes ma'am." He escorted them to the house, making them wait on the porch while he searched the house and barn thoroughly. A few minutes later, he came outside, shaking his head. "I think he's gone."

A familiar truck came barreling up the drive and jerked to a halt beside the cruiser. Peter jumped out. "Take me through the sequence of events," he said to Kate after the obligatory greetings. They all went out to the greenhouse. Kate showed Peter and Deputy Webb the fan, explained what she had seen, and pointed out the bolt. Then she led the way down to the stream. There they found new prints, pointing back across the ditch and onto Slim Baker's land.

"The footprints were only coming in before," Kate said. "It looks like he left finally." The vista in both directions was empty of anything living save a few grazing steers, who ignored their presence.

Peter bent over and peered at the prints. "The soil is kind of wet, but let's try to get casts of these prints, Webb. Take photographs first, though." He straightened and turned to Bebe. "I'm going to have experts look at that fan to see if they can validate what happened. I agree with Kate that the bolts were loosened, and whoever did it knew the fan would fall when it kicked on."

"How did he know someone was going to be standing under it?" Kate asked.

Peter shrugged. "Maybe he just took a chance."

Bebe chewed at her lower lip, thinking. "I have a theory. I spend a lot of time out there midday, which is around when the automatic fans turn on. Perhaps they knew that."

Who would know that? Someone who used to work for Bebe, perhaps. She took a deep breath. "Bebe, can you tell me why you fired Phoebe?"

Bebe folded her arms across her chest and frowned. "Surely you don't think she had something to do with this?"

"I understand why you're reluctant to think someone you know means you harm," Kate said slowly. "I've grappled with that at times myself. But someone obviously does."

Bebe gestured at the long shoe prints Webb was photographing with his digital camera. "Those aren't her footprints. She's tiny."

Kate glanced at Peter, and she knew he was thinking the same thing: If Phoebe was involved, she wasn't working alone. Kate was grateful when he stepped in to back her up.

"Bebe, at this point we have to look at everyone," he said, his voice gentle. "If she's innocent, then she'll be ruled out. But someone who knows your schedule planned this ... accident."

Kate realized with a jolt that if the fan had hit Bebe, it might have been ruled just that—an accidental malfunction of equipment. How clever. They hadn't banked on Kate being there with her suspicious mind.

"All right." Bebe blew out a breath. "I was trying to do Derek a favor by hiring her. I guess no good deed goes unpunished." Her lips quirked in a rueful smile. "I caught her snooping through my personal papers. Bank statements and the like."

"Do you think Derek put her up to it?" Peter's tone was mild.

Bebe rubbed her forehead with a thumb and index finger, as though soothing a headache. "I hate to think that. Yes, he owes me money, but he's never been that devious." She added a qualifier. "At least not that I know about."

So, Derek was acquainted with Phoebe, and earlier that day they had been at the same place. Kate knew that much. Were they plotting Bebe's demise, or was it for another purpose? Kate decided she would tell Peter later what she'd seen at the gas station. She remembered something. "Bebe, I think you should show Peter the threatening letter you got."

"Yes, I would like to see it," Peter said. "Kate mentioned it the other night."

"It's in my file cabinet," Bebe said, turning and walking up the path. "Filed under *E* for 'enemies.'"

Peter gave Deputy Webb additional instructions and advised him to call in a forensics team. Then he and Kate walked to the house. Bebe was coming downstairs from her office when they arrived in the hall. She handed the warning to Peter; it had been stored safely in a plastic sleeve as Kate had suggested. "It's probably got my fingerprints all over it, but maybe you'll be able to get something."

He took the sleeve and studied the letter. "Of course it's

typed. Everyone who watches television now knows how to make an anonymous threat, so I'll bet they wore gloves. I'll have forensics check it out anyway."

Bebe sank down onto a step. "Do you think I should cancel the retreat? Besides this attack on me, we've still got Sylvester Vink to worry about." She raised her brows. "Unless you've caught him. That would be one less thing to worry about."

Peter shook his head. "He's surprisingly elusive. We did find an abandoned stolen car in a parking lot in Magnolia Creek, so it appears he's moved on to a different vehicle."

"Have you heard from Mary Benson yet?" Kate asked. "I suggested to Paige this morning that if she's at the women's shelter, she should let you know."

"We haven't so far. So you think that's where she is?" Peter's glance was admiring. "I usually warn you to stay clear of these investigations, but good work."

Kate felt a warm rush of pleasure. "It made sense. If Vink abused her, she was trying to hide from him. When her cover was blown here, she probably went somewhere secret. They're so locked down, they don't even give out the address."

"Good thing," Bebe said. "Maybe I should go there myself." Her tone was wry. "So, any advice regarding the retreat? I'd hate to put my guests at risk."

"You could hire a security guard," Peter said.

Bebe's face fell. "True. But having hired muscle around will spoil the mood, I'm afraid. Oh, by the way, the security company will be out here this afternoon. They said they'll definitely be finished before the retreat."

"That'll help, but it won't prevent people from prowling around the grounds." Peter rubbed his chin. "I have an idea." He paused and stared into space. Then he pulled out his phone and checked his calendar. "Yes, I think it will work."

"What is it, Peter?" Kate felt like stamping her foot in impatience but refrained.

"I'll stay here undercover." He bowed. "Ma'am, meet your new hired hand."

Kate liked that idea. It would be wonderful to have Peter around to prevent any more "accidents." She'd felt so much better the night before, knowing he was downstairs.

Bebe eyed him speculatively. "Can you cook? I could use some help in the kitchen." She rose from the stairs. "In fact, I'm going to make lunch right now. We can test your skills."

Peter laughed and held up a hand. "No, I'm afraid I'm a hopeless cook. All I can do is grill meat and fry eggs and bacon." He shrugged. "And burn toast."

"How about yard work?" Kate said. "You could pose as a gardener."

"True," Bebe said. "There's always a lot of outdoor work to do around here." Her brow creased. "Of course, I can't ask you to actually do the labor." She began to walk toward the kitchen, gesturing for them to follow.

"You should see what I've done for jobs while undercover." Peter straightened his shirt cuffs. "A little raking and weeding is nothing."

"Tell me more about your undercover work," Kate said as they entered the kitchen, which had retained an old-fashioned charm despite shiny new appliances and cream granite counters. She went to the stainless fridge to pull out the meat and cheese she'd purchased. Bebe washed ruffled lettuce and then sliced bread while Kate put together the sandwiches.

Peter perched on a stool at the counter. "Let me check in with Deputy Webb first." He made a quick call. "The forensics team is here. I'll have to eat and run," he said as Kate placed a ham-and-cheese sandwich in front of him. He picked up a half, took a bite, and gave them a thumbs-up. "OK. One thing I did was work at an oil field as a roughneck. That was for a murder." He took another bite, chewed and swallowed. "Drove a garbage truck investigating an organized crime ring. And, of course, I've done an obligatory drug sting or two."

During Peter's recitation, Bebe glanced at Kate and raised her brows as if to say, "See, he does like the adrenaline."

"That all sounds very exciting," Bebe said. "Let's hope your stint as a groundskeeper is entirely uneventful."

"Part of me hopes so," Peter said with a grin. "But I don't mind a little action if it means we close a couple of cases." He wiped his mouth with a napkin. "Thanks for lunch. I'd better get outside and check on the team."

"I'll help clean up," Kate said. "And then I'd better get to work."

"Me too," Bebe said. "I still have tons to do before the retreat starts."

Kate cleared the plates, rinsed them, and put them into the dishwasher while Bebe wiped down the counter with a damp cloth.

They were finishing up when someone knocked on the back door, located off the kitchen in an annex used to hang coats, the type of room people in Maine called a mudroom. "That's probably the security company."

"I'll get it," Kate offered. But instead of the installers, Peter stood there. "Hello again. That was quick."

"They found something I want to show Bebe." He held up a clear evidence bag. "This was underneath the table crushed by the fan." It was the tassel from a man's leather shoe.

She'd seen that tassel before, or one just like it, on a pair of shoes worn by Derek Morehouse.

Fourteen

Bebe joined them at the back door. Her face paled when she saw the tassel. "That looks like Derek's."

"That's what I thought," Kate said. Although she knew she needed to keep an open mind, she hated to think that Derek would try to harm his generous ex-wife. Besides, loafers hadn't left those prints by the stream, and surely the person who had was the one guilty of sabotaging the fan.

"He'd never wear those shoes in the mud," Bebe said, echoing Kate's thought. "And no way would he try to kill me. I'll never believe that."

"Maybe he lost the tassel off his shoe days ago," Kate said. "Right, Peter?"

Peter's tone and face remained carefully neutral. "I'll have to ask him about it, of course. But yes, everyone's innocent until proven guilty in my book." He turned to go. "They're almost finished out there, so you can have someone repair the fan whenever you want, Bebe." He gave them a little salute. "I'm heading home to pack a bag. I'll be back later."

That evening, as she sat on the porch with her friends, watching the sun set and eating a dinner of barbecue chicken and sweet potato salad, Kate reflected that she was really enjoying all this socializing. Yes, she relished—even needed—solitude in order to design and create, but it was all too easy to get used to being alone, to the point where she resisted seeing people. She smiled fondly at Vivi, who was telling a spirited and amusing story about demanding clients to the great entertainment of the others.

Peter shook his head. "Better you than me. I'd probably tell them off and get fired."

"You deal with worse every day," Vivi pointed out. "Actual criminals."

"Yes, but I can arrest them and lock them up."

"Touché." Vivi laughed. "All we can do is charge them extra." She rubbed her palms together. "A lot extra."

"I'll have to keep that in mind," Bebe said. "The difficult guest surcharge."

"You have to call it something else," Vivi advised. "VIP service."

Peter grinned. "Good one." He glanced down at his empty plate. "I guess I wolfed that down. Shall I do the dishes?"

"Yes," Kate said, handing him her equally clean plate. "I was going to offer but since you did ..."

"I rented '70s TV shows on DVD for tonight," Vivi said, adding her plate to the stack. "When you get your chores done, you can join us."

"Thank you kindly, ma'am," Peter said with a slight bow.

"That's 'miss' to you," Vivi said crisply. "I'm too young to be a ma'am."

"I stand corrected, miss." Peter bowed again, to everyone's laughter.

The retreat center had a big-screen television. So, after making popcorn and lighting a fire to take off the evening chill, they settled down to enjoy *Charlie's Angels* and *The Mod Squad* to inspire Kate's designs and get ideas for the fashion show. Even better, they shared lots of laughs over the dated dialogue and plots, a welcome break from the stressful events of the past few days. When Peter armed the alarm before sending Kate and Vivi up to their rooms, Kate was certain she would finally get a much-needed full night's sleep.

The next morning, Kate was on the staircase when she overheard Peter talking.

"Captain, I told you I would take personal time." His tone was strained, as if he was attempting to keep irritation under control.

Unless his boss is down there, he is on the phone. She turned to go back upstairs rather than barge in on a private conversation, and a tense one at that.

"No, it won't interfere with the interagency project. Check out Bluebonnet Farm on the map ... you'll be thrilled at where I am."

Despite her efforts to block her ears, Kate clearly heard his words. She didn't know if she was more surprised that Peter was staying here on his own time or that there was an important investigation underway. To keep from hearing more, she deliberately began to hum, then went into her room and closed the door. What should she do? Her gaze fell on her crochet class project. She'd do that for a few minutes, long enough for Peter to finish his call.

"Darn it." With her mind on other things, she bungled a whole row.

"Having a bad day already?" Vivi, still in pajamas, appeared in the doorway of the connecting bathroom.

Kate set the project aside. "I shouldn't try to crochet before coffee."

"Wait for me? I'll just be a few minutes." At her nod, Vivi closed the bathroom door.

Since Vivi wasn't going to the office and could skip full makeup and hairstyling, she was showered and dressed in record time. When they went downstairs, Kate saw Peter had left. She hoped he didn't realize she'd overheard his phone call, even if it was by accident. Rather than pry, she preferred to let people tell her what they wanted her to know. Except when she was investigating bad guys, of course.

As they walked up the path, Vivi clutched Kate's sleeve to stop her progress. "Is that who I think it is?" Her eyes were wide with excitement.

Kate studied the tall man lounging on the porch beside Peter, both of them cradling mugs. She certainly did recognize that handsome face topped by a mane of sun-bleached brown hair. A Stetson hat was set carefully on the table next to his knee. Texas Ranger Sam Tennyson, solver of cold cases and Vivi's Prince Charming.

"What's he doing here, I wonder?" Kate said. *Is he part of the interagency project?*

"That's what I want to know." Vivi put on a burst of speed as she strode the rest of the way to the porch steps. "Hey, Sam. You here for a yoga class?" Her grin was wide and teasing.

"Vivi." Sam stood, his face a comical mix of emotions. "Yoga? What's that? No, I'm here …" His voice trailed off and he glanced at Peter.

"He stopped by to talk about one of my cases," Peter said. "Isn't that right, Sam?"

"Yes, that's right. I'm sure glad to see you, Vivi." His gaze moved to Kate. "And you too, Kate." He cleared his throat. "I understand you've been having some trouble around here, so Peter's staying on-site?"

"That's right." Kate stopped at the screen door. "I'm going in for coffee. Who wants breakfast?"

Everyone accepted the offer. As Kate entered the house, she heard Vivi invite Sam to the barbecue she and Kate had been planning. Despite Vivi's denials, Kate knew her friend was quite enamored of the good-looking and well-mannered ranger. She didn't blame her a bit.

Kate didn't think Sam had just happened to stop by. The Texas Rangers were only involved in the most complicated and high-level cases. In light of Peter's comment to his boss, she reframed Peter's evasion when she'd first mentioned Slim Baker during lunch at the Thai restaurant. Then there were the incidents at the farm, trying to get Bebe to sell. And Phoebe, Bebe's ex-employee, and Derek, her ex-husband, together at one of Slim's gas stations. She should mention that to Peter since it seemed like everything was connected in a way she couldn't quite figure out. Were they all connected to the bigger case Peter and Sam were working on? She had a feeling the answer was yes.

In the kitchen, Bebe was pulling a pan of homemade biscuits out of the oven, releasing the homey odor of fresh baking. "How do egg-and-cheese biscuits sound? I also have sausage patties." A platter of cooked turkey sausage sat on the stove.

Kate poured herself a cup of coffee. "That sounds great. I'll help." She sipped her brew while gathering plates and silverware. Bebe beat eggs and made a big omelet she cut into rounds for the biscuits. Kate helped her assemble the piping-hot sandwiches.

"Just in time," she said as Vivi came into the kitchen. She

handed her two plates, paper napkins tucked underneath. "These are for the guys."

"Do you believe Sam is here?" Vivi's eyes were glowing. "I'd almost forgotten how gorgeous he is."

Bebe cocked a brow. "He'd be a hard one to forget. Peter too. If I'd known policemen were so handsome, I wouldn't have focused on rock stars and millionaires." Her tone was droll.

Vivi laughed. "They're especially good-looking when you need one." She winked and sashayed out of the kitchen, holding the plates high.

Kate settled down to crochet after breakfast, surprising herself by her progress despite all the distractions. Vivi and Bebe were down the road at a farmers market, making last-minute purchases for the retreat menu. Peter had reluctantly left for a meeting, promising Kate he would ask the sheriff's office to send Deputy Webb by on patrol and that he would return as quickly as possible. Sam had taken off on a ranger assignment, but to Vivi's delight, he had promised to come to the barbecue they were planning for later in the month.

After finishing the scalloped edge of the dress hem, she slipped it onto the mannequin to see how it draped. The garment hung in lovely folds with the floral design falling in the proper place across the upper chest and waist.

Alexus should see this. Kate picked up her phone and took a few shots from various angles. Then she put the camisole top she'd finished on the form and photographed that too. In addition to wanting to share her progress, she also knew it wouldn't hurt to get her editor's blessing as she went along. Her nightmare was working for months, then having her designs rejected.

She downloaded the photos onto her laptop and saved them in the project file. Then she pulled up her email and composed a message. Should she tell Alexus about Ariel modeling her designs and Derek's offer to photograph the illustrations? Both were pretty exciting and would probably help the book sell. Another idea floated into her mind. It would be beyond wonderful to have both Bebe and Ariel as models, maybe even on the cover. She could picture them posed in the flower garden, backlit so their pale hair glowed, wearing her gorgeous crochet garments.

Her fingers hovered over the keyboard as she debated. Her immediate impulse was to run the idea by her editor, who had the power—and the budget—to say yea or nay.

But she should probably wait. Ariel was a lovely person, but the jury was still out on Derek. He—and his shoe tassel— seemed to have a habit of being in the wrong place at the wrong time. She sent the email without mentioning the couple and then put the dress back on the form, debating whether or not it should be a tad longer.

Vivi poked her head in. "We're back." Her gaze fell on the dress and she gasped. "That is gorgeous, Kate."

"You think so?" Warm pride swelled in her chest. "Thanks."

Vivi circled the dress, looking at it from all angles. "Just stunning. I can't wait to see it on a live model."

Voices in the hall caught Kate's attention. She heard Ariel's high-pitched twang and Derek's booming English accent. "You won't have to wait long, I'm guessing," Kate said. "My model has just arrived."

Their hostess insisted it was time for lunch—she'd made

tomato soup and goat cheese bruschetta—so they gathered in the kitchen for the meal. Afterward, Kate found herself sitting on the porch, waiting for Ariel, who was making phone calls. Vivi and Bebe were still in the kitchen, and Derek was off somewhere. Her heart rose when she saw Peter walking along the path from the barn; she was glad to see that he was back. Then she noticed he was wearing work clothes and carrying a shovel. Instead of his usual cowboy boots, he had on work boots.

"I see you're taking your undercover role very seriously." She couldn't hold back a smile.

"Go ahead and laugh." Peter thrust the shovel into the dirt of a flower bed. "I'm great at digging holes, I'll have you know."

"I'm sure. It's what you do next that's the question."

Peter laughed. "I think I'm planting these." He pointed to several plants in pots. The screen door squeaked open behind Kate, and he turned and began to dig.

With a sigh, Derek took the rocking chair beside Kate. His glance at Peter was dismissive, a sign that Peter's disguise was effective. He was invisible, like many service workers.

"How are you, m'lady?" Derek asked, rocking vigorously in his chair as he stared out at the garden. He was wearing the loafers again, and yes, one tassel was missing.

"I'm great. In a few minutes your wife is going to try on the clothes I've made. I really appreciate having her help." They rocked in silence. "How are things with you?" she asked politely.

Peter had completed one hole, and he bent to remove a plant from its pot. Kate sensed he was listening, noting the alert position of his head.

Derek sighed again. "It's hard work getting an agency off the ground. I'd forgotten that."

"Finding clients, you mean?"

He glanced over with raised brows. "Oh, no. I have plenty of clients. I need to find more talent." His eyes lingered on Kate, taking in her face and what he could see of the rest of her.

She shifted in discomfort. "Surely there are tons of pretty girls around Fort Worth." Texas was famed for leggy, big-haired beauties who became cheerleaders, models, and pageant winners.

"Yes, there are." A flirtatious tone crept into his voice, not overt enough for Kate to take offense but bold enough to make her squirm. Peter grunted as he slapped the soil into place around the recently planted flower a little harder than necessary.

"You can't be talking about *me*." Kate tried to sound dismissive, as if it was the most ridiculous thing she'd ever heard. And it was, almost.

"Why, yes I am." Derek scooted his rocking chair a little closer and leaned over to speak confidentially. "Not every model needs to be twenty years old, six feet tall, and blond, you know."

The shovel clanged, and when Kate glanced over, she saw a frown on Peter's face. He quickly turned his back and pretended to focus on digging another hole by shoving the implement in with a fierce thrust.

Kate laughed with a chuckle that sounded false to her own ears. "Is that so? What kind of job would I get? Displaying household cleaners?" She thought of the women in old advertisements wearing dresses and aprons, their nails and hair perfect.

"Exactly. A lot of local companies want women who represent their typical customer. A very attractive one, of course." He nodded as he checked her over again. "You'd be perfect. Driving a car. Working in an office. Giving snacks to kids."

Despite her general dislike at being the center of attention or having her photograph taken, Kate couldn't help but feel flattered. This man had made women world famous, after all. Maybe he did know what he was talking about. The extra money would certainly come in handy.

"I'm not photogenic." She shook her head. "Believe me."

"That's because you've only been photographed by hacks." He tapped his chest. "Trust *me*."

The loud crunch of breaking plastic caught their attention. Peter was stamping on one of the plant pots, apparently trying to loosen the soil.

"I guess you can't get good help these days," Derek muttered. He shifted in the chair and dug in his pocket. "I've got a card in here somewhere. Let's set up a test." As he withdrew his hand, the contents of his pocket clattered onto the floor. A pen. Coins. A wooden disk rolled away and ended up under her chair.

Kate got out of her chair and reached between the rockers for the disk. She grabbed it and pulled it out. It was the eagle-embossed coin she had seen in the gas station, the one the attendant hadn't wanted her to examine too closely.

Fifteen

"I'll take that," Derek snapped, reaching out his hand for the wooden coin.

She dropped it into his palm. "What is it? Toy money?" Maybe he would be more forthcoming about it than the clerk. Didn't they realize their reluctance only aroused curiosity?

"Something like that." He didn't make eye contact as he shoved everything back into his pockets. He patted them again. "I guess I don't have a card on me. I'll get one for you later."

Ariel stepped out onto the porch, and Derek quickly went to greet her with a kiss on the cheek. "There you are, my love. Getting ready to do a little modeling?"

"I'm ready if you are," Kate said as she made a mental note to tell Peter about the eagle coin.

The other woman shrugged elegantly. "Let's do it."

In the studio, Kate had Ariel try on the camisole top first, which looked perfect with the slim jeans she was wearing. The model turned this way and that in front of the full-length wall mirror. She stretched out one arm and then the other while Bebe and Vivi looked on.

"I really love this, Kate. All my friends will too." She fluffed her blond hair and made a pouty face at herself in the mirror.

"Wow, Kate, I'm impressed," Bebe said. "Who would have guessed these retro styles could look so fresh again?" She spun around and looked at the dress on the stand. "I have an idea. Let me put on that top, Ariel. You get into the dress."

"What are you thinking, Bebe?" Ariel looked puzzled.

"We're going to model these garments for our friend." She looked at Vivi. "While we change and do our faces, would you ask Derek to set up his camera, please?" She tapped her chin, considering. "In front of the rose arbor. The 'Lady Banks' is blooming."

Kate blinked, not sure she was hearing correctly. The idea she'd had earlier was coming to life right in front of her eyes.

Watching Derek photograph the models was an education in itself. By the time they arrived in the garden, he had set up the camera and tripod, lights, and diffusing umbrellas. First he had both of the women move around in the garments so he could see how they looked from different angles. He made adjustments to the lights and umbrellas and then moved them into position in front of the lush yellow roses spilling over the arbor.

"What's going on?" Kate turned to see Peter, still in his work clothes.

She greeted him with a smile and a finger to her lips. "We're watching a real photo shoot," she whispered.

"They don't even look like the same people," Vivi whispered back. Indeed, the two women were also in professional mode, their focus and poise making them seem somewhat otherworldly as they moved.

In contrast, the scowling man who suddenly thrust his meaty head and shoulders through the bushes behind them was all too real.

"Move out of the way, please." Derek flapped his hand at the man interfering with his shot, apparently not realizing he was a wanted criminal. The models looked at Derek, puzzled. "Not you, him." He pointed. "Go on, get."

"That's Vink," Kate said with a gasp. Daylight didn't improve the man's coarse features and stringy hair.

"I see that." Peter's face was grim as he withdrew his gun from its holster and sprinted across the grass.

The man turned and thrashed through the bushes. The models screamed and ran out of Peter's way.

"The gardener carries a gun?" Derek's mouth dropped open in confusion.

"Get inside, everyone," Peter ordered. To Vink he yelled, "Police! Stop and put your hands up!" Pulling out his phone with his other hand, he called for backup.

"Is that the man who was in your room?" Vivi asked.

Kate shuddered. "Yes. I hope Peter catches him this time."

"I guess we're all done for now, ladies," Derek said dryly as Bebe and Ariel ran toward the house. "And the session was going so well." He began to unscrew his camera from the tripod.

"Do you need some help, Derek?" Kate asked, fighting the urge to run screaming toward the house herself.

Derek placed his camera in its leather case and slung the strap over his shoulder. "If you grab the tripod, we can resume shooting inside. I have another light, so the rest of the equipment can stay out here for now."

Kate quickly released the legs of the tripod, not bothering to shorten the legs all the way. She tucked the long, somewhat awkward poles under her arm and hurried after Derek and Vivi. The path back to the house led between banks of flowering bushes. The others were out of sight around a corner when Kate felt something pull on her leg and stop her progress. Certain she had gotten hung up on a bush or branch, she turned around.

Sylvester Vink was standing right behind her.

Cold fear rooted Kate to the spot.

Vink grabbed the tripod, tugged it out of her arms, and

threw it onto the grass. Then he lunged forward and wrapped a thick arm around her neck. "Don't say a word or I'll cut you."

To her horror, Kate felt the point of a sharp object digging through her shirt into her ribs. All the air left her body and her knees sagged. Was he going to kill her? She closed her eyes and prayed. *Please, no.* Thoughts of Vanessa danced in her mind.

"Let her go, Vink." Peter's voice was calm and authoritative.

Hope revived Kate slightly, and she opened her eyes to see Peter a short distance away, his gun trained on them.

"No way. Let me go or I'll cut up your little girlfriend." He underscored his words with a slight movement of the knife that made Kate cry out. "I mean what I say."

"Kate!" Vivi had come back to find her friend. She stood in the middle of the path, hands to her mouth in horror.

"Stay back, lady," Vink said. To Peter he said, "I just want to get out of here. Do what I say and no one gets hurt."

"Except Mary," Kate blurted. Her reward was a tightening of Vink's hairy forearm. She tried to duck her chin, wishing she could reach down far enough to bite him.

"Shut up." Vink moved sideways, propelling Kate along with him, her feet dragging and stumbling. "Move back, cop boy. You too, lady. Go stand next to him where I can keep an eye on you."

Peter stepped backward, his gun still trained on Vink. Kate knew he wouldn't risk a shot that might injure her. Vivi ran to stand behind Peter, despair on her face. Kate noticed her eyes darting around and knew she was trying to think of a way to help.

"I've got more officers on the way, Vink," Peter said. "You won't get far."

"You better hope I do or she's going to pay." Vink gave

another yank on Kate's neck, this one vicious. He pulled her down the path.

Kate began to choke as the pressure increased on her throat. Squeezing her eyes shut, she concentrated on pulling air into her lungs. Her arms and legs went numb, and a rushing noise thundered in her ears. Was she going to pass out? Or die?

Sixteen

The rushing noise in her ears turned into a series of squawks followed by a yell. Suddenly, the arm around her neck was gone, as was the knife. Kate collapsed to the ground, landing heavily on her side.

She rolled over onto her back and opened her eyes. Tansy was attacking Vink, who had tucked himself up into a ball. "Get it away from me!" He batted at the chicken with one hand and covered his head with the other. In a flurry of feathers, Tansy continued pecking while Vink bellowed and tried to fend her off.

The knife lay near Kate, a gleam of silver in the grass. Peter kicked it farther from Vink's reach and pulled out handcuffs. "Lie flat on the ground and I'll get rid of the chicken." A smile quirked his lips, but he managed not to laugh at the sight of the valiant bird flogging the larger man.

Vivi ran to Kate's side. "Are you all right?" Kneeling down, she helped Kate sit up.

Kate rubbed her bruised throat. "Yes. I think so," she croaked.

Vink lay facedown on the grass, and Peter was fastening his wrists with handcuffs. As he read the man his rights, two sheriff's cruisers arrived. The fun was over, but Tansy was still clucking frantically nearby.

"That chicken may have saved my life," Kate said. "Peter couldn't do anything as long as Vink was holding a knife on me."

"I wonder why she attacked him," Vivi said. "It was amazing."

"Bebe said she acts like a dog. But maybe it has something to do with that." She pointed. Under a bush near where Vink had been standing was a little nest of dried grass. In the middle, a smashed egg oozed yellow.

"Oh. Poor Tansy."

With his prisoner secure for the moment, Peter came over and helped Kate to her feet, one arm remaining around her. "Are you all right?"

"I'm fine." Her voice cracked again, and she cleared her throat. "Or I will be once I get something to drink."

"I'll call for an ambulance and have them check you out," he said. "I have to take care of processing Vink." He gazed into her eyes. "I'm so sorry you went through that." He squeezed her shoulders. "And relieved everything turned out OK."

"Me too. I guess he circled back around and I happened to be there." She attempted a smile. "I hope Mary Benson will be safe now."

After a gentle hug, Peter released her with a pat on the shoulder. "Once I add attempted kidnapping to the other charges he's been racking up, Mr. Vink won't be free to bother Mary or anyone else for a long, long time."

Vivi helped Kate to the house, where they found the others gathered in the comfortable living room, Bebe and Ariel on a sofa, and Derek standing in front of the mantelpiece. As they entered, Bebe jumped up. "Are you all right, Kate?"

"I'm fine," she croaked as Vivi guided her to a vacant sofa. "Just a little shaken."

"Vink grabbed Kate and tried to kidnap her at knifepoint," Vivi said. "He was hoping to use her as a hostage."

Ariel and Bebe exclaimed in shock, and Derek swore softly under his breath.

"Vink is the creature who was lurking in the bushes, I assume," Derek said. "I couldn't imagine what he was doing, popping up like that in the middle of my shoot." He frowned in annoyance.

"He's been stalking Mary Benson," Kate said, one hand to her throat. "The woman you all know as Martha Brown."

"The woman who was hit on the head?" Ariel's face went pale. "Thank goodness you caught him."

"Actually, Tansy helped." Vivi walked to a window and peered at the driveway. "Oh, good. The police are taking Vink away now. And here come the EMTs."

"What do you mean, Tansy helped?" Bebe asked.

Vivi told them how Tansy got the jump on Vink after he stepped on her nest, giving Peter the chance to arrest him without risking injury to Kate.

Bebe gasped in amazement at the hen's antics. "I always thought Tansy acted more like a dog than a chicken. This just confirms it. I'm never getting rid of her."

"I guess this means you won't sell her to me," Kate joked. "I wanted to use her as a watch-hen."

The medical professionals knocked on the front door, and Vivi hurried to answer.

"So, explain something to me," Derek said to Bebe. "I gather your gardener is a moonlighting policeman? How odd."

Bebe glanced at Kate, who subtly shook her head. It was better if Bebe didn't tip off Derek—or anyone—about Peter's true purpose of protecting her. "He's a friend of Kate's, here to help us for the weekend."

"A man who was in the right place at the right time, then." Derek picked up his camera case and walked over to give his wife a kiss. "I'm going to pack up my equipment and head home. Give me a call later, love."

The others followed Derek out of the room, giving Kate privacy with the EMTs, a man and a woman. After checking her over thoroughly, the man said, "No permanent damage I can see." He unwound the pressure cuff from around her arm. "Take it easy tonight. You'll be good as new tomorrow."

Someone tapped on the door, and the female EMT answered. It was Peter.

"It's OK. Let him in," Kate said.

"We're going to head out," the woman said, grabbing the medical equipment. "Have a good night."

"Thanks for your help," Kate said as they departed. "I thought you left," she said to Peter.

"I wanted to check on you first." Peter hunkered down beside her chair. "How are you feeling?"

"Better." She rubbed her neck for what seemed like the hundredth time. "It's not hurting as much."

"No one would blame you if you went home."

"I don't want to miss anything." She pushed herself out of the chair. "Besides, what would I do at home all by myself?" She leveled him with a look. "You're coming back and staying, right?"

"Yeah, that's true." Peter rose to his feet and pulled his phone out to check the time. "I'll be back as soon as I finish the paperwork."

"Come to my class if you want. It's at seven tonight." She smiled at the thought of the lanky policeman sitting with a group of women and working on a crochet headband.

"No way." He tapped her nose with a forefinger then gave her a quick kiss. "See you later."

The festivities began around four, when several luxury vehicles pulled into the driveway. Ariel, who had neglected to take off the crochet dress, ran barefoot down the path to greet her friends, followed by their hostess. Five young women spilled out of the vehicles, talking and laughing and hugging.

Bebe herded them up the path to meet Kate and Vivi, waiting on the porch. "Kate Stevens is one of your instructors this weekend. She made the dress Ariel is wearing."

Many "oohs" and "aahs" and "Where can I get thats?" followed.

"I'm a designer, not a dressmaker," Kate protested. Inwardly she was elated at the admiration her creation was receiving. Something else to tell Alexus. If wealthy, stylish women wanted her designs, then crochet was definitely moving away from being perceived as old-fashioned and frumpy.

Vivi was introduced as co-hostess. As such, she showed the women to their rooms so they could unpack and get ready for the classes before dinner, stretching, and aromatherapy. Kate went to the kitchen to help Bebe, who was baking chicken breasts and putting together a huge salad for dinner. The breasts would be sliced on top of the greens and garnished with homemade sesame ginger dressing.

"This looks fantastic," Kate said, admiring the colorful mix of spring greens. She sliced scallions and sprinkled them on top.

"I grew most of it." Bebe opened the oven door, pulled out the pan of chicken, and set it on the stove. "Good thing the fan didn't crush my lettuce." Although her tone was flippant, Kate saw tension in the line of the older woman's shoulders.

"I'm glad it didn't crush *you*," Kate said.

"Me too." Bebe stripped off her oven mitts and tossed them onto the granite counter. "Usually cooking relaxes me. Today I'm all wound up." She took a deep breath and stretched her arms wide. "I need to take my own advice."

"I totally understand." Kate flapped the front of her T-shirt.

"My heart still hasn't settled down from what's happened the last couple of days."

"You are one brave woman, Kate Stevens." Bebe's eyes shone with sincerity.

I sure wasn't considered brave back in Maine, she thought. *Have I really changed that much?* "I just do what I have to do."

"Well, I think you're amazing." Bebe picked up a cardboard pint of grape tomatoes and tipped them into a colander. "Maybe I should have cancelled the retreat. I keep thinking something else will go wrong." She set the colander in the sink and turned on the spray.

Kate could understand that. Yes, Sylvester Vink was taken care of, but there was still the question of who was threatening Bebe. "I think Peter has things under control." She hoped so. "And Vivi and I will be keeping our eyes open."

Bebe turned off the water. "You two have been invaluable. And in return, I'll do whatever I can to help." She smiled. "For one thing, I'm going to spread the word about your designs to everyone I know in the fashion world." She picked up the colander and shook it. "And that's a lot of people."

Kate's knees sagged in a familiar feeling of shock, this time in response to something good. What was the definition of grace she'd recently heard? "Unmerited favor," that was it. "You are too kind," she murmured as she took the colander.

While sprinkling tomatoes on the salad, she remembered someone who was waiting for news. She should call Paige and tell her Sylvester Vink had been arrested. Maybe now Mary Benson would dare to come out of hiding.

One case down, one to go.

After dinner in the spacious dining room, the ladies adjourned to the retreat center for Kate's class. She passed a basket of yarn and hooks, allowing each student to pick the colors she favored. Even though they were adults, she'd found that colored hooks added an element of fun.

"I'm warning you, I'm all thumbs," a redhead said, selecting emerald-green yarn and a hook. "I can't even thread a needle."

"Can you tie a knot?" Kate gave her a reassuring smile. "We'll take it step by step." At her nod, Vivi moved to sit near the woman. She was going to be Kate's aide.

"My grandmother did this," another said, a blonde who chose blue yarn. "But until I saw the dress you designed, Kate, I thought crochet was ugly."

"It can be," Vivi said. "Pea-green hats, anyone?" Everyone laughed.

A brunette fingered a length of red yarn. "I think this is a great idea. Headbands will look perfect with our workout gear." She gestured at the others, who were all wearing yoga pants and tops, mostly black.

"I read that doing crafts has a similar effect to meditation," Bebe said. "And that's why I asked Kate to teach this class."

"I think I saw that," someone else said. "Doing handcrafts also helps fight depression and stress."

"Sounds like exactly what I need," the redhead said. "And since you do it with your eyes open, I can watch my three-year-old twins at the same time." The women laughed again.

Kate led the group through the instructions while she and Vivi provided hands-on help when required. Ariel was the only one not joining in the fun, Kate noticed. She sat away from the group, tucked into a soft chair near the fire, her gaze on the flames. Her pale pink headband lay in her lap, only a couple of rows finished. "Are you stuck?" Kate asked.

Ariel shook her head. "No. Just daydreaming." She picked up her work and began to hook again but not before Kate noticed traces of tears on her cheeks. Something was definitely troubling her.

Deciding it wasn't the time or place to probe, Kate turned back to the group. Bebe had set up teapots and plates of presumably low-calorie cookies on the big table, so Kate announced a break. "We're going to have refreshments now, so you can either keep going or work on your project again tomorrow. Vivi and I will be around all weekend if you have questions."

The redhead yawned extravagantly. "I'm ready for bed. This class worked wonders. Thanks, Kate. And Vivi." The rest of the women clapped before getting to their feet and beginning to chatter and mingle.

Bebe was serving the chamomile tea Kate disliked, so she declined and slipped outside to see if Peter had returned. His truck was parked near the barn, but she didn't see him anywhere. He'd avoided the class, she realized with a smile. But he was somewhere on the grounds.

She circled around behind the house, a rising moon shedding light on the path along with little solar lights tucked among the bushes. The farm had so many enchanting nooks that she hadn't explored yet. Following the sound of a fountain, she emerged from a boxwood hedge into an open area. Low lights framed a cherub sitting with birds, water pouring from his hands. The sound of sobbing drew her attention to the far side of the clearing.

A woman was tucked up in a swing, hands over her face. As she drew closer, she recognized Ariel. Kate had been right; she was upset.

"What's wrong?" Kate asked gently, sitting on the swing beside her.

"Everything." Ariel sobbed louder.

She didn't tell Kate to go away, so Kate sat waiting for

Ariel to cry it out. A figure stepped out of the bushes nearby and stood watching. Peter. She gave a discreet gesture for him to leave and that she would talk to him later. He nodded and slipped back into the darkness.

Finally Ariel's sobs slowed and then stopped. She scrubbed at her face with her hands, brushing away the tears. Kate dug around in her pocket, found a clean tissue, and handed it to her.

"Thanks." Ariel dabbed her eyes. "Sorry about this."

"Hey, we all need to cry sometimes."

That neutral but sympathetic statement opened the floodgates. "It's Derek. I'm so worried about him."

"He told me he was working hard getting the agency going. Is that what you mean?" Perhaps his health was suffering. He wasn't exactly young.

Ariel shook her head violently, her blond hair swinging. "He's worried about money, especially since I've been nagging him about having a baby." She sniffed as tears welled up again. This was obviously a topic close to her heart.

Kate gave her a moment. "He's doing something you don't approve of to get money?" she guessed.

"Yes. He's gambling again, I think." She gave a short laugh. "He thinks it's the easy way to raise a bunch of money. He's good at it, but things can go the other direction pretty quickly." She wiped her nose daintily. "That's why he went bankrupt years ago. One of the reasons, anyway."

The wooden eagle coin came to mind. Was it a gambling chip, similar to the ones used by casinos? If the gas station was an illegal gambling den, that would explain so much. The strange customers. The clerk's reaction to her comment about the coin. Derek Morehouse stopping there. And Phoebe. What was her role in all this?

Seventeen

Kate stood in front of the chicken coop, basket in hand. When Bebe asked her to collect eggs, it had sounded like a pleasurable early morning chore. There was only one problem: She couldn't find a way into the coop, which was tucked inside a screened area filled with milling chickens. The small wooden building had no door and was accessed only by a ramp barely big enough for poultry.

"Good morning."

She looked up to see Peter, dressed in his gardening clothes, striding along the path from behind the barn. "Do you know how to get the eggs out of there?"

Peter laughed. "Fortunately I do. Otherwise I can just see you trying to crawl inside." He waved at her to follow.

They walked around to the rear, and Peter lifted a hinged board. "Voilà." Clusters of eggs lay inside the hay-lined box.

"The chicken coops I saw in Maine were more like barns. You could go inside and reach under the chickens to get the eggs." Kate grabbed one of the warm brown eggs. "So they lay them inside and the eggs roll out here? How convenient." She glanced up at Peter. "How did you know that?"

"I had egg duty on my grandmother's farm." He reached for a white egg and placed it gently in the basket. "There's nothing as tasty as fresh eggs, that's for sure."

After they gathered almost two dozen eggs, Peter took the basket out of her hands and set it on the ground. He wrapped his arms around her. For a long moment, she relished the safe, warm feel of his embrace. "We've never spent so much time in the same place but had so little time together," he said.

"I know." Kate rolled her eyes in mock irritation. "Between capturing criminals and helping with the retreat, I've barely seen you." She glanced around, relieved not to see anyone else out enjoying the fresh morning air. "And before we're interrupted, I have a lot to tell you." She quickly filled him in about seeing Phoebe and Derek at the gas station, the wooden coin Derek had in his pocket, and what Ariel had said about her husband's gambling. While she talked, Peter paced back and forth while the chickens scurried from one side of the coop to the other in tandem with his movements.

Kate broke off her story and laughed, pointing at the hens. "Look. They're following you."

Peter halted and so did the birds, an inquisitive one or two pressing close to the fence. "That's because I've got grain in my pocket." He opened the door and threw corn onto the ground. The chickens jostled each other aside in their haste to get to the treat first.

"You are such a softy."

He looked sheepish. "Yeah, I guess so." His tone of voice sobered. "Listen, Kate, please be careful. Until this is wrapped up, it's hard to say who can be trusted."

"You mean Derek and Ariel."

"Afraid so."

She hated hearing that, but she supposed he had a point. She picked up the basket. "I'd better get these to the kitchen. Bebe needs them for breakfast."

He fell into step beside her as she headed for the back door, the silence between them fraught with what remained unsaid. Kate sensed something big was underway but that he couldn't tell her anything right now. She really didn't want to pry into police matters anyway. It was bad enough she managed to get involved in every case that came her way. She had a knack for attracting trouble, it seemed.

After omelets for breakfast, the retreat guests and Vivi went into the garden for classes taught by Bebe. Peter had another mysterious meeting, so Kate took the opportunity to sketch her next design, a lace-crochet button-up blouse that would look superb with dressy skirts or pants. Since the design was open, she'd pair it with a peach or pink silk camisole underneath. Pale blue or green would look good too.

After a couple of false starts, she hit upon a combination of design elements that made her fingers tingle, a sure sign she was on the right track. Setting aside her pad, she rooted around in her bins and bags for the soft ivory thread she wanted, but she couldn't find it.

After checking her inventory once again, she remembered she had filled two bags at Once Upon a Yarn. But only one was there with her. Maybe the other was still in the van. She pictured it behind the front seat, on the floor perhaps.

A rapping on the front door startled her, making her drop a cone of thread. Still crouching, she glanced up and saw a woman standing there. A woman in her fifties with long blond hair.

Kate hastened to open the door. "Mary Benson?"

The woman's eyes were wary. "Who wants to know?" She was pretty, but her closed expression spoke of a woman used to guarding her thoughts and feelings.

"I'm Kate Stevens, a friend of Bebe's." Kate omitted mention of Sylvester Vink and her role in his capture, sensing that his name would upset the woman. Paige must have passed along the message, or maybe Mary heard the news of her ex-boyfriend's arrest. In the interest of discretion, she didn't ask.

"Nice to meet you." Mary gave her a brief grimace of a smile before her face fell back into its customary reserve. She craned her neck, gazing around the studio in curiosity. As her hair swung out, Kate caught a glimpse of a white bandage. "Is Bebe around? I have something to tell her."

Kate's senses sharpened. Had she remembered something about her attack? "I think she's teaching a class in the garden. Would you like to wait?"

Mary shifted from foot to foot, hesitating. "I don't know ..."

Kate smiled warmly, trying her best to reassure the obviously nervous woman. "How about waiting on the porch? I'm sure she'll be done soon." She tried not to appear too eager and scare her off. If Mary went into hiding again, they might never find her.

"All right." Mary frowned. "But I don't have long."

Kate let out her breath. "I'll go tell Bebe that you're here."

She left Mary perched on a rocking chair and dashed through the garden to find Bebe. She hoped she would be at a good stopping place and could come right away. The woman reminded her of a skittish stray cat—forlorn, distrustful, and likely to bolt at a sudden movement.

Bebe was strolling barefoot between the rows of students, all of whom were lying flat on mats with their eyes closed, Vivi among them. "Deep breaths," she said. "Take deep, slow breaths and release all the tension from your neck" When she spotted Kate hovering on the edge of the clearing, she came over. "What is it?" she whispered.

Vivi opened one eye and peeked at Kate, then closed it quickly when Bebe glanced her way.

Kate spoke into Bebe's ear so as not to disturb the students.

Bebe held up a finger in the universal "one minute" gesture before ambling back to the group. "Now feel the tension rising up through your chin, your ears, the top of your head. Breathe deep and release." She crouched down next to Vivi and whispered instructions. Vivi nodded and sat up just as the redhead next to her began to snore. Vivi shot Kate an amused look.

"That woman is certainly relaxed," Kate said as Bebe rejoined her. They hurried up the path, Bebe having caught her sense of urgency.

"On any given day, some of them do go to sleep. With their overbusy lives, they need the rest, I guess."

Kate sighed. "You'll have to teach me that. I often have trouble sleeping."

"Be glad to. It's called the corpse pose."

Kate smiled at the less-than-cheerful name. They came around the last corner and she scanned the porch. No Mary. But Kate found a note sitting on the chair, which was still rocking gently back and forth.

"I just wanted to say I'm sorry. Martha/Mary."

Bebe held the note, her brow creased in bewilderment. "What could this mean? *I'm* the one who needs to apologize. She was hit on the head by someone who thought she was me!"

"Sorry for bringing Vink into your life, maybe?" Still, Kate wasn't sure how much Mary knew about what had happened with Vink. "Bebe, exactly when did Mary take over for Phoebe?"

Bebe tapped her lip, thinking. "The day after I fired Phoebe. Actually, I'd barely put up the ad when she called. Her background as an executive assistant was perfect."

"Did she say why she left her last job?" Kate remembered from the résumé she'd only been in it a couple of months.

"She said something about the company being sold. I guess a lot of people lost their jobs."

Kate spotted a brightly colored canister sitting on the table by the rocker. "It looks like she left you a gift too." She handed it to Bebe.

Bebe looked pleased. "This is my favorite tea. She must have remembered." She tucked the tin under her arm and opened the screen door. "When you see Vivi, tell her I'm putting together a snack to eat during our nutrition class. I'll need her help to take out the trays."

Kate could barely restrain her excitement while waiting for Vivi. She sent her rocking chair into a frenzy, her mind whirling with what could be another dead end. But the pulse leaping in her veins told her otherwise.

Finally she saw Vivi's blond head approaching through the bushes. "Do you have a minute?" she called.

"A couple," Vivi said. "They're taking ten before our next class. What's up?"

"Something really odd just happened. Come with me while I look something up on the Internet, and I'll tell you about it."

"How can I say no to that offer?"

Vivi followed Kate to the studio where she filled her in while booting up her laptop. "This won't take long, I promise." Kate's fingers flew over the keys. "I just want to check the ownership of Eagle Oil Products." She typed the name in the business name search section on the Texas Secretary of State website.

"That's a pretty wild theory you came up with," Vivi said, crossing her arms as she leaned back against the table. "Based on a one-sentence note, no less."

"You know me. Give me half a clue and I'll give you a wild theory." Kate scanned the list of business names that popped up. "Let me see. Yes, this looks right." She hit the keys again to bring up corporate documents.

Vivi leaned down to look over her shoulder. "The registered agent is Brendan Oliver. Isn't that—"

"Yes. The same attorney who registered Worthy Stores and More Models." Kate swung around on the stool to face her friend. "And I didn't find any press or information about Eagle Oil being sold recently. If it had been, new corporate documents would have been filed."

"So, Mary was lying about losing her job," Vivi said slowly.

Kate grinned in triumph. "Yes. I bet someone sent her to work for Bebe. Someone connected with either Derek or Slim Baker."

"Or both."

"I have an idea." Picking up her phone, Kate plugged in the contact number from the corporate filing for Brendan Oliver. "I'm calling that attorney."

"Won't he know it's you?"

"Nope. I blocked my ID." She put the phone on speaker so Vivi could hear.

"Hello," a man's gruff voice answered, followed by the honking sound of nose blowing. Kate did a double take, having expected a more formal response. Had she dialed the right number?

"Good afternoon. I'm calling for Brendan Oliver." She put on her version of a high-class, snooty voice. Vivi stifled a grin behind her hand.

"Brendan Oliver speaking." He sounded stuffy, and he sniffed loudly to punctuate his words. So attractive.

"Oh, I wasn't sure I had the right number." Kate was making this up as she went along, her thoughts only one step ahead of her words. "I was wondering if you could help me with ... um, a business matter."

"Of course. That's my specialty, business law. Incorporations, dissolutions, financing, tax planning—"

Kate sighed deeply. "My dear Walter recently passed away. He had quite a portfolio, you know. But I'm just not sure ..." She deliberately let her voice trail off.

"Sorry for your loss," he said, his voice perfunctory. "But I don't handle estate matters."

"Oh, no, you misunderstand me. I want to use my inheritance to buy a business."

He cleared his throat. "How much are you, er, thinking of, Mrs. ...?"

"Mrs. Holden." She used the name of her crochet mentor back in Maine. "Mrs. Elizabeth Holden. I was thinking somewhere in the neighborhood of ten million."

The man audibly gulped then coughed. He must have been drinking something. "That amount will give you a range of options." He coughed again. "What type of business are you interested in?"

"Oil. Walter always said you couldn't go wrong with petroleum. The other day I heard about a nice little company that just came on the market. Eagle Oil Products."

Dead silence was followed by a choked reply. "May I ask where you heard that?"

"I don't remember."

Another silence. "You heard wrong, I'm afraid. Eagle isn't for sale. However—"

Kate cut him off with a crisp thank-you and goodbye. "He didn't like hearing that. Probably wondering where the rumor started."

"So we know Mary was lying. The question is, why?"

"I think she was sent to spy on Bebe," Kate said, lowering her voice. "The police have something big underway." She told Vivi about the conversation she'd overheard between

Peter and his boss. "I think that's why Sam was here. The rangers are involved too."

Vivi mock-pouted. "Is that why he was here? I thought he was tracking me down."

"I'm sure seeing you was a bonus. Anyway, I'm guessing they're staking out Baker's property next door."

"There's more going on than a contentious land deal, then."

"That's what I figure." Kate glanced at the time. "Oops. Didn't you have to go?"

"Yes." Vivi scooted for the door. "Why don't you join us?"

Kate decided she needed a break and went to the class, which was very informative. Bebe told them to focus on including a variety of healthy foods in their diet rather than fixate on what they should avoid. "If you fill up on fresh vegetables and light proteins and whole grains, you won't want that extra cookie or slice of cake," she said.

"How about my addiction to chocolate?" the redhead said. "I've been known to raid my kids' Halloween and Easter stashes." The others laughed.

"Often when we crave caffeine or chocolate, we're trying to give ourselves a boost. If you keep your blood sugar stable and get lots of sleep, you'll find your cravings go away."

"You mean get lots of sleep during yoga class?" one of the others said. Everyone laughed again, and the redhead blushed.

"If that works for you, go for it." Bebe gave her a reassuring nod. "That's it for this class, everyone. Next, we're going to have another exercise class, a gentle blend of martial arts I created."

Kate skipped that and spent the rest of the day in the studio, working on the blouse. At about four in the afternoon, she joined Bebe and Vivi in the living room for tea. The students had free time to rest or relax before dinner.

"Did you have a productive day, Kate?" Bebe asked. She

picked up a teapot. "Would you like a cup? It's the gift Mary left me. Imported English."

"Sure. I'll try that."

Bebe poured three cups of steaming tea, and Kate and Vivi doctored theirs with milk and, in Vivi's case, sugar. "Give it a minute to cool. It's still really hot."

"Today was really fun," Vivi said, setting her cup and saucer on the table next to her chair. Her cheeks were glowing from the fresh air and exercise. "I feel great." She wiggled one shoulder, then the other. "And I'm not as tense as usual."

"I should try one of the yoga classes tomorrow," Kate said.

"We're having the men join us for the last session, so that'll be a fun one," Vivi said.

"That's right. Maybe I can get Peter to join me." Kate grinned at the thought of him contorting his long limbs into yoga poses.

"We're also having a photo session with Derek before lunch for those who want one," Bebe said. "He's giving us a discount because I think he's trying to line up more local models." She picked up her cup and blew gently on the liquid.

"He was even trying to talk me into it." Kate made a face as she picked up her own cup and took a tentative sip. It was tepid enough, but it tasted rather bitter.

Kate hastily set her cup down with a clatter and leaped toward Bebe as she put the cup to her lips.

"Don't drink that!"

Eighteen

Bebe jerked her hand. Tea went everywhere, all over her lap, the chair, and the rug. Wide-eyed, she stared up at Kate. "What are you talking about?"

Kate hovered next to her, feeling somewhat foolish. But she'd also learned to rely on her instincts. "Something's wrong with it. It didn't taste like any tea I've ever had."

Vivi smelled her own cup, her lips twisting in a grimace. She set her cup down hastily. "She's right. It doesn't even smell like tea."

Bebe reached for a napkin and dabbed at the spilled tea on the chair. "Maybe it's a bad batch. I'll get rid of it."

Kate and Vivi exchanged glances. "Bebe, I think you should give it to the police. I'm thinking it might have been tampered with." Kate grabbed another napkin and pressed it onto the wet spots on the rug. Vivi did the same.

Bebe paused in mid-swipe. "You mean poison? Why would Mary give me poisonous tea?"

"We don't know who left the container," Kate pointed out. "We're just assuming it was Mary since she was here. Someone else could have sneaked onto the property and put it on the porch."

"Did anyone else know it was your favorite?" Vivi asked.

"Who *doesn't* know? I've gotten that tea for Christmas and my birthday for years. I even mentioned it on my blog." Despair washed over her face. "This is horrible." Her lips trembled and tears welled up in her eyes. "Someone really does hate me."

Kate couldn't deny that, considering the rest of the incidents targeting Bebe. But she attempted to reassure her friend. "We don't know if it's poison for sure. Let's give it to Peter. He can have it tested."

When Peter arrived back at the farm, he took possession of the tea container, now safely sealed in a plastic bag. "Never a dull moment," he grumbled to Kate. "I told my captain I shouldn't leave at all, not until everything was over." He quickly ducked his head after this last comment, as if he'd said too much.

They were alone in the studio she had set up at Bebe's, so she boldly asked, "Why don't you tell me what's going on, Peter?"

He seemed intent on writing on an evidence bag with a marker. "I don't know what you mean." He capped the pen, slid the tea into the evidence bag, and sealed the top.

Kate ticked off the clues on her fingers. "One. Sam was here. Why? You know rangers only do big cases. Two. The eagle coin I saw at the gas station and in Derek's possession says to me that Slim is, or was, involved in illegal gambling. Three. Brendan Oliver, Slim's—"

Peter put up his hand. "Hold it. What's that about Brendan Oliver?"

Kate explained how she'd learned that Brendan Oliver was the attorney of record for the Worthy chain of gas stations and Derek's agency. "He also filed the paperwork for Eagle Oil Products, the company where Mary Benson used to work. So I bet Slim is involved with them too. He's from Houston, you know, and his real name is Elmer."

Shaking his head, Peter sagged down onto the stool in front of the worktable. "Kate, you never cease to amaze me. You put two and two together faster than some of the trained detectives on my team."

"So, Slim Baker is running gambling joints?" Kate felt a thrill of vindication. Her instincts were on target.

Peter gestured at the half-open door. "Can you close that, please? I don't want anyone to overhear this."

Kate hurried to the door, glancing both ways down the hall before shutting it. No one was in sight. She knew Bebe and Vivi were working on a shrimp-and-rice concoction for dinner in the kitchen, and the guests were still enjoying their rest period. As she turned back into the room, she saw several women strolling past in the garden, laughing and talking. She checked the French door to make sure it was fully shut.

"OK, Peter. Spill." She stood with legs planted wide, arms crossed.

Admiration slid across his face as he regarded her determined stance. "Yes ma'am. First of all, I am here to keep an eye on you all, not that I've succeeded so well at that."

"You caught Sylvester Vink," Kate said. "That was big."

"No, Tansy did." He tried to suppress a smile.

"I think you should recommend her for a hero's medal." Her eyes met his and they both burst out laughing. Kate imagined the chicken at an awards ceremony along with people who rescued babies from burning buildings and so forth. "All right, go on."

Peter sighed. "Slim Baker has been under surveillance for months and under suspicion for far longer. The vice squad suspects he has ties to organized crime, but no one has been able to pin anything on him. He's one of those guys who comes out of nowhere, sets up a business, and boom, they're spending money hand over fist. Something doesn't add up."

"Money laundering?" Kate knew that certain types of cash businesses were fronts to funnel the proceeds of crime into legitimate channels.

"Absolutely. The gas stations were perfect. Hold gambling operations in the back room and then deposit the cash in the bank, claiming it's from selling sodas and snacks."

"So he sold the chain before he could get caught?"

"Not exactly. He still owns them, but now he's a silent partner. At least that's what our forensic accountants figured out. Plus, he got a bunch of cash out of the deal to develop the motor sports park at the property out here."

"Which will be another front?" It seemed to Kate's admittedly inexperienced eyes that the racetrack would attract lots of interest in gambling, much like a horse track.

"We think so. Actually, we think he's already using it that way now. That's why we're staging a sting tomorrow night."

Someone knocked on the door and, without waiting for an answer, opened it. "Whoops." Vivi put a hand to her mouth when she saw Peter. "I'm sorry. I didn't mean to interrupt. I didn't know you were back, Peter."

"It's OK, Vivi," Kate said. "I was telling him about the tea. He's sending it to the lab."

"The case of the toxic tea." Vivi shook her head. "Anyway, dinner is ready if you guys want something to eat."

"We're right behind you." As Kate started to walk toward the doorway, Peter touched her arm and put one finger to his lips. "Got it. No one will hear a peep out of me."

Dinner was outside in the garden, under the pergola, which was strung with tiny white lights. A line of candles marched down the middle of the table, and fragrance drifted both from the surrounding garden and bowls of cut flowers on the tables.

It should have been incredibly romantic. But Peter was eating in the house alone since he was pretending to be the gardener. Kate was left listening to eight women chatter about topics that seemed terribly trivial compared to the issues weighing on her mind. Of course, Bebe and Vivi silently shared her concerns and occasionally caught her eye, their expressions letting her know they were worried too. But they—especially Bebe—put on a good front so as not to spoil the retreat.

"Can we have another lesson after dinner?" one of the guests asked Kate. "I'd love to keep working on my headband."

The others joined in with a torrent of pleas and Kate found herself agreeing to teach again.

It wasn't until after class that Kate saw Peter again. She, Bebe, and Vivi were still sitting in the main room of the retreat center. The rest of the guests had gone upstairs.

"Hey, Peter, look what you missed." Vivi adjusted the blue headband she wore around her head. "We finished our nifty headbands tonight."

He pretended to do a double take. "Can I get one in camo? The guys down at the station would be so jealous."

"Actually, they do make yarn in camo colors," Kate said, keeping her face deadpan as the others laughed. Noticing that Bebe had shifted forward in her chair, an anxious look on her face, Kate asked, "Any news on the tea?" Peter had sent it to the crime lab via deputy courier.

He shook his head. "Not yet. Bebe, I'd like you to sleep in

this building tonight. Easier to keep an eye on one building rather than two."

"I have two beds in my room," Vivi said. "Why don't you bunk in with me, Kate?"

"As long as you don't snore," Kate said, trying to keep things light. "I need sleep."

"I can make you some chamomile tea," Bebe offered. She pushed herself to a standing position. "I'll get fresh sheets for Kate's room, if that's all right with you, Kate? I hate to displace a guest."

"Not a problem, really. I was just joking. And please, don't bother with tea." She gave a big, half-fake yawn. "I'm exhausted."

Despite her words, Kate found herself wide awake an hour later. There hadn't been an opportunity for more than a quiet conversation in the hall with Peter, who said they would talk in-depth after the retreat ended the next morning. A million thoughts racing through her mind, Kate sat up and pushed the covers back. If she didn't do something, she would jump right out of her skin.

Vivi lay still in the other double bed, but Kate couldn't tell if she was sleeping.

"Vivi, are you awake?" she whispered.

"No. Are you?" Snickering, Vivi rolled over on her side to face Kate. "My mind keeps going over everything."

"Mine too." Kate thought for a moment. She couldn't discuss the police sting, so she settled on the other puzzle consuming her. "The situation with Mary is really bothering me."

"I know. At first I thought she was just in the wrong place at the wrong time. Then we learn she's on the run from Vink. And now we know she worked in a business connected to Brendan Oliver, who in turn is connected to businesses Slim Baker owns. Or owned."

"I couldn't have put it better myself." She wanted badly to tell Vivi the rest of the story, about the coin and the gambling, but she managed to restrain herself. Kate got out of bed and padded across the room.

"What are you doing?" Vivi sat up and turned on her bedside lamp, wincing in the sudden glare.

"I have my laptop. I think we should do a little research."

"Into Mary?"

"And Slim Baker. After I saw that note, I couldn't help but think that Mary was sent as a plant." She slid the computer out of her tote and carried it back to the bed.

"You don't think she was apologizing for the tea?"

Kate laughed. "That would be a new one. Apologize in advance for trying to kill someone with your present." She booted up the computer.

Vivi snickered again. "That tea was the perfect example of a killer gift." Her face sobered. "Sorry. I get silly late at night."

"So do I." Kate tapped away on the keys.

"What are you looking for, exactly?"

"I'm trying to see if I can connect Slim and Mary somehow. It seems odd that a woman in Houston would be selected to come up here and spy for him."

Vivi snapped her fingers. "They're about the same age, right?"

"I think so. Let me find a bio of Slim." Conveniently, one had been posted on the Eagle Motor Sports Web page. "Let's see. 'Elmer—'"

"Elmer? His real name is Elmer?" Vivi giggled. "No wonder he goes by Slim."

Kate smiled as she scanned the page. "He was born and raised in Houston. After high school, he began his career working in the oil fields." She looked up. "So, Mary and Slim are both from Houston."

"Maybe they went to school together. Or worked together."

"Let's hope it was school. We don't have Mary's real work history." Kate searched a high school reunion site for Elmer Baker's name. There wouldn't be too many Elmer Bakers in Houston, she hoped. Finally she hit pay dirt. "Slim's class had a reunion last year and he was the guest speaker."

"Let me see." Vivi perched on the bed beside Kate. "'Local man gives keynote about business success.'" She pointed to the senior picture of Slim in the sidebar. "I guess that's why they nicknamed him 'Slim.'" The photo depicted a scrawny, pimpled boy with wide sideburns. "He's changed a lot."

"That's for sure." Kate scrolled down to find the list of attendees. "Bingo." She pointed. The list included "Mary (Baker) Benson." "There she is. And look at her maiden name."

Vivi's eyes were wide. "Baker! Is she his cousin, maybe?"

"Baker is a fairly common name. But I think that's a very odd coincidence."

"You know what they say." Vivi's voice was comically authoritative and deep. "There are no coincidences."

Nineteen

Everyone rose early the next morning for a yogurt-and-fruit breakfast served outside to sounds of twittering birds. Sitting on the swing under the rose arbor, Kate was both exhausted and keyed up. She had experienced this state before, at the end of cases when all the loose ends and unanswered questions were on the verge of being resolved. Once the one or two missing pieces were located, the puzzle would be complete.

Peter entered the clearing and sat beside her, holding an egg-and-sausage sandwich. "Good morning, Kate."

"Morning." Kate noticed Peter wore sweatpants, a T-shirt, and a pair of sneakers. "You're not dressed in work clothes."

He leaned close, and she caught a whiff of aromatic aftershave and shampoo. His hair was still damp and curling up at the ends. "I'm going to join the yoga class this morning."

She pulled back to look at him. "You're kidding."

"Nope. I thought I'd see for myself what all the fuss was about." He took a big bite of his sandwich.

Laughter bubbled up inside her. "That's great. I can't wait." She ate a spoonful of lightly sweetened yogurt and blueberries. "Are we still on for tonight?"

"As far as I know. Once everyone clears out of here, we can talk more about it."

"Vivi and I found some significant information online about Mary Benson last night."

"What was it?" The sound of several cars pulling up

the drive attracted his attention. "Looks like we've only got another couple of minutes."

"Mary and Slim Baker went to the same high school. They might even be related. We're not sure. Her maiden name was Baker. We think Mary might have been a plant, a replacement for the snoopy Phoebe."

"And then she got beaned on the head and was off the job."

"It might explain that note she left. She felt remorseful since Bebe had been nothing but good to her."

Peter crammed the rest of his sandwich into his mouth and wiped his lips with a napkin. "You could be on to something," he said after he finished chewing. "Let's talk later."

The arrival of the men turned the retreat into more of a social function. There was coffee and more breakfast food on the porch along with a lot of chatter and laughter. Bebe gave tours of the gardens, and the women displayed their headbands, quite cute with their black yoga togs. The men wore sweats and T-shirts much like Peter's. Even the elegant Derek had abandoned his beloved tweed jacket and loafers for workout clothes and sneakers.

The yoga mats were placed in lines in the grassy clearing. Bebe had everyone choose one, alternating men and women. She started off with deep breathing and the soothing yet invigorating stretches of the sun salutation sequence. Then she led the class through a series of poses that were deceptively simple yet required muscle.

Kate, in the very back between Vivi and Peter, watched the proceedings with amusement. She'd overhead one man saying before class that standing in one position after another was easy and for wimps. That same man now grunted and strained as he held his body in place.

"I take back what I said, Bebe," he wheezed as they moved

to an easier position. "Anyone who can do this is amazing."

Everyone laughed. Bebe frowned at first as yoga was supposed to be an intense and quiet discipline, but she gave up and allowed the class to make comments and cheer one another on. She even had Peter come up front and demonstrate the tree pose, which involved standing with one foot tucked into the opposite thigh, arms overhead.

"See how still he stands, all parts in perfect harmony?" Bebe nodded for Peter to come out of the pose. "You have great balance, Peter."

"Of course he's good at the tree pose; he's young," Derek said.

"Is there a money pose?" the first man asked. "I'm a banker."

"I'd like one that brings money to you," said another.

Bebe broke up the banter. "We're going to do the undertaker's favorite pose: the corpse. Lie down, everyone." Of course, this suggestion was met with great hilarity.

Peter had placed his phone on the grass between him and Kate before they started the session. Now it dinged, and without thinking, Kate glanced at the text on the screen. "Tea tested positive for cyanide."

Eyes closed, she lay flat again. But Bebe's soothing instructions couldn't penetrate her whirling thoughts. The tea had been poisoned. Had Mary tried to kill her former boss? Or had she merely been an unwitting courier? There was always the possibility that someone else had brought it to the farm.

At long last the class was over. Then there were photography sessions and lunch to get through. Finally, at about two o'clock, the cavalcade of cars filled with satisfied guests pulled away with waves and smiles, Kate, Bebe, and Peter sending them off.

"Thank goodness that's over." Bebe sighed, her shoulders

drooping. "I think I'm going to sleep for a week." She shot a look at Peter standing nearby. "Any news on that tea?"

He compressed his lips. "Yes. I want to talk to you about that and some other things." He turned to Kate. "Where's Vivi?"

As if conjured by his words, Vivi came out of the retreat house, lugging her suitcase. "I'm heading out. I've got a big day tomorrow. What are you up to, Kate?"

"I'm going to work here awhile. I'll be home later." She had no intention of leaving. She felt compelled to keep Peter's operation a secret, but she hated misleading her friend.

Vivi gave her a mischievous smile. "Don't work too hard." She laughed, and Kate realized Vivi thought she was making excuses to spend time with Peter.

"I won't. And let's get together soon to discuss the barbecue menu."

"Definitely." Vivi opened the door of her Mini Cooper and thrust the suitcase onto the backseat. "Goodbye, everyone."

"I'll be in touch about planning another retreat," Bebe said, coming to give her a hug. "I couldn't have done it without you."

"I'm looking forward to that," Vivi said, patting her new friend's shoulder. "Take care."

"Hold on a minute, Vivi," Peter said. "How would you like to help with an undercover operation?"

Vivi's eyes lit up. "Oh yeah, I would." She glanced back and forth from Kate to Peter. "I knew something was up."

"What do you think?" Bebe asked, gently combing the top layer of Kate's hair into place. She picked up a can of hair spray and blasted it all over.

"I think I look like a beauty pageant contestant," Kate said. Bebe had teased her shoulder-length hair into a huge flip and caked her face with a deep layer of foundation, blush, eyeliner, mascara, eye shadow, and lipstick. She reached one hand to her cheek. It felt like her skin had been spackled. Would it crack if she smiled? She tried it to see.

Vivi giggled. "You look awesome. Just like a high roller's trophy wife."

"That's the idea." Bebe set down the hair spray. "I have a silk shirt you can wear with your jeans. With lots of jewelry and your cowboy boots, you'll look just right—casual but expensive."

Kate had dashed home to get her own boots since Bebe's wouldn't quite fit. She'd also stopped to pick up jeans that were double the price of what she usually spent. The bonus was that they were extremely flattering.

"Uh-oh. I didn't think about jewelry." She hardly ever wore it.

Bebe opened a box on the dressing table. It was filled with gold and silver chains, earrings, and bracelets. "I have plenty." She pulled out several chains and hoop earrings. "These will be perfect."

"Thanks so much for doing this, Bebe," Kate said. "I had no clue how to make myself look like a different person."

"It's the least I could do to help you and Peter," Bebe said, meeting Kate's eyes in the mirror with a smile. "I'm glad my skills were useful, even if in a small way."

Peter stood when Kate entered the living room in her outfit, his face revealing shock and amusement. "Wow. Is that really you?"

She twirled to let him admire the entire effect, feeling the pull of the wire attached to her bra as she did so. Vivi had helped wire her for sound and video since she and Peter would be monitored by police while they were undercover.

"You look quite ... amazing yourself," she said, checking him over.

Peter wore a fake mustache and goatee and what she assumed were nonprescription glasses. Wearing a big cowboy hat and fancy duds, he was practically unrecognizable. The swagger as he came toward her completed the impression of a middle-aged Texas businessman. "Ready to go, little lady?" Even his accent was stronger and his voice just a little deeper.

"Good luck, you guys," Vivi said at the front door.

"Your job is to keep an eye out until we get back," Peter said. "If anything happens, anything at all, text me." He handed her a throwaway phone. "The number is entered as 'Butch.' And make sure the house alarm is set."

Vivi glanced out the door at the sheriff's car parked in the yard. "Is he staying too?"

"Yes," Peter said. "I'm not taking any chances with anyone's safety. Hopefully after tonight, this whole ordeal will be over."

As Peter helped her into the Lexus SUV he'd rented for the night, Kate hoped with all her heart that he was right.

It wasn't far to Slim Baker's property via a direct route, but Peter took the long way around. He wanted to pretend that they were coming from Fort Worth. With every mile they drove, Kate's nerves increased, winding so tightly she thought she might scream.

"Peter—" she began, but then stopped, unwilling to say

more. He'd probably drop her off back at the house if she had a meltdown.

"It's OK, Kate," he said. "Think about who you are. Myrna Adams, a very attractive socialite out for an evening with her good-looking husband." In the dim light of a streetlight she saw him wink. "It's what I do. Otherwise I'd go nuts before a mission."

"You pretend you're Myrna?"

That broke the tension, and they both laughed. Finally he turned onto Slim's drive, which was wide and well-groomed dirt. He pulled to a halt at the first gate, which stood open but was guarded by two armed men. Peter gave their false names, Butch and Myrna Adams, and the guard spoke into a radio. Receiving an affirmative, he nodded for them to proceed.

Once they were inside the property, another man indicated where they should park. Quite a few cars were there already, among them a Mercedes and a huge black Hummer. Was it the one Tansy had adorned? Kate couldn't tell in the dark.

The event was being held in a large barnlike structure nearby, as was evident by the lights and music spilling from a door as it opened and closed. Otherwise, there were no windows. Or, if there were any, they were shuttered tightly, an indication of illicit activity.

Two more guards stood near the door. Peter handed them the wooden eagle disk as their admission ticket. Kate had been right that it was connected to gambling. Then they were both frisked. Kate held her breath in fear that the man would feel the wire running down her belly to the transmitter inside her pants. But the pat-down was cursory and apparently aimed at finding weapons.

As she preceded Peter into the building, Kate's gait hitched at the realization that he wasn't carrying his gun. They were truly dependent on their wits and a wireless connection to police backup.

"Are you all right?" Peter whispered into her ear, his hand firmly on her lower back.

"I'm fine. I almost tripped." Kate quickened her steps. They passed through a small anteroom with a coatroom and another guard sitting behind a counter, staring at a bank of security cameras.

The large main room echoed with music and the noise of revelers talking, laughing, and cheering. Along one wall was a bar; tables nearby were filled with patrons eating and drinking. The middle of the room was filled with roulette wheels, craps and blackjack tables, and a bank of slot machines. Near the bar, television sets mounted on the wall were tuned to various sporting events, gamblers keeping an eye on the outcomes.

Staff dressed in black slacks and white shirts roamed the room or stood at the tables, dealing. A girl with distinctive spiked hair sauntered by. *Phoebe.* Her presence was proof she had been working for Slim Baker all along.

Kate touched Peter's arm to get his attention as the girl wove her way through the tables. "Phoebe Newland," she whispered into his ear.

He nodded in understanding. "Let's go over to the bar. I want to talk to Slim for a minute."

"What should I do?" She was afraid to expose herself to Slim's scrutiny in case he recognized her.

"Why don't you go play a game?" He gave her a box of gambling chips. "Try to keep a low profile."

Kate had never gambled and had no idea what to do. But a tall, thin dealer in a leather vest spotted her. "Come on over, pretty lady. Try your luck tonight." When she hesitated, the other players at the craps table joined in and encouraged her.

"All right," she said with a toss of her hair, which of course didn't move an inch. "You'll have to show me how to play."

They made room for her at the oval table. When the present shooter lost, the dealer told Kate where to place her chips and then handed her the dice.

"Shake them."

"Blow on 'em."

"Say a prayer."

The suggestions came at her fast and furious from bystanders.

"Just throw them hard enough so they hit the far wall of the table," the croupier said.

Kate threw the dice. When they came to rest, everyone cheered. Following instructions, she rolled again and again, and she kept winning.

Her streak accomplished the opposite of what Peter had suggested as a strategy, and soon spectators were crowding the table to watch.

"I thought you were a novice," the dealer said, shaking his head ruefully.

"I am," Kate said. "Cross my heart." She made the gesture. "I guess it's just beginner's luck." She glanced toward the bar where Peter stood talking to Slim. Their discussion was taking much longer than a few minutes.

"Give me some of that," another man crowed.

"Them dice are hot tonight," someone else said.

A woman wearing the white blouse of an employee pushed through the crowd to stand beside Kate. Light perfume floated off the woman's long hair as she flipped it over her shoulder. Shaking the dice cupped in her hand, Kate glanced over at her and their eyes met.

Mary Benson.

Twenty

A shock jolted through Kate. This was not good.

By the widening of Mary's blue eyes, Kate knew she had been made. She tossed the dice and, to the groans of the crowd, lost. Her streak was over, and so was her undercover stint. She stepped back from the table. *What should I do?* If she went over to Peter, Mary would know he was with her.

She glanced back over her shoulder. Mary wasn't looking her way. In fact, she was running across the floor in the other direction, jostling people out of her way. *To fetch a security guard?* She should tell Peter what was up, and then they could get out of there.

Slim was talking, Peter listening intently. By the satisfied curve of his lips, Kate guessed Slim was spilling the beans. "As you can see, this operation is going to be very profitable for everyone involved."

"I can see that. It's very attractive." Peter edged slightly closer, lowering his voice. "But I heard you were having problems with an adjacent landowner. What's the deal with that?"

Kate froze, her ears straining to hear Slim's reply. How clever of Peter to get Slim to talk about his campaign against Bebe.

Slim laughed and clapped Peter on the back. "You'll be happy to know it's being resolved. Tonight, as a matter of fact."

Peter noticed Kate standing there. "Hey, darlin'. How are you?"

Kate tugged at his sleeve. Slim's words had only increased

her urgency to escape. "We need to get out of here," Kate whispered into his ear. "Now!"

With a finger held up to Slim, Peter took Kate aside. "What's up?"

"I've been made. And we have to get back to the farm. Didn't you hear what Slim just said?"

"Don't worry about it. Webb is there, remember?"

Just then the phone in his pocket beeped. He pulled it out and stared at it, then showed it to Kate. The message on the screen was brief: "Help."

"You're right." Peter grabbed Kate's hand and moved toward the door.

Then a bullhorn blared. "Freeze! Everyone is under arrest."

Instead of obeying, the crowd did the opposite. It was mayhem with yelling and screaming and people thronging toward the front door. A team of police came bursting through from that direction, sending the crowd back into the room.

"What the heck? They're not supposed to be here." Pulling Kate along behind him, Peter bulled his way through the milling, panicking mass of people to the men's room. Inside, he barged through a stall door and pushed open a window over the toilet.

"How did you know where to go?" Kate said, gasping. Her heart was pounding, fit to burst out of her chest.

"Rule one. Always locate alternative exits."

In the main room, screams and yells increased in volume as the police began to round everyone up. "Get up on the toilet," Peter urged her.

Her legs shaking, Kate obeyed. Feeling like she had somehow ended up in an action movie, she allowed Peter to push her up and through the window. Fortunately, there wasn't a long drop to the ground, and she landed on her feet.

She jumped to one side as Peter landed next to her.

"Run." He took off and she followed, forcing her legs to obey. They had ended up behind the barn, and Peter led them into the dark fields. The route to their SUV was cut off by the squad cars and vans.

"Police! Stop and put your hands up!" A man's voice boomed through the dark.

Peter came to halt, his boot heels skidding in the dirt, and raised his hands. Kate copied him. "I'm Detective Peter Matthews. Fort Worth PD."

A flashlight shone in his face, making him squint, then moved to Kate's face. "Can you prove that?"

"I'm undercover, deputy. No ID."

"Check us out," Kate said. "We're wired."

"The vice team busted an undercover op?" The deputy sounded skeptical.

"Tell me about it." Peter's tone was ironic. "What a mess-up. With all of this going on, I don't know if any of my people are headed this way or not."

"What you got there, deputy?" A man approached, swinging his flashlight beam on the ground.

"Got someone here says his name is Detective Peter Matthews. Fort Worth."

Another beam played briefly over their faces. "Yep. That's him." The man grunted a laugh. "Nice 'stache, Matthews." He lowered his light. "Let 'em go."

"Now that's cleared up, we need backup at Bluebonnet Farm." Peter waved the phone. "Just got an SOS."

The two deputies exchanged looks. "We'll try to pull someone away." The second man headed across the grass toward the building.

"Let me use your flashlight." Peter held his hand out to

the first deputy. "We're going across the fields, not through that mess." Blue and white lights were strobing in the front of the barn, and the babble of voices and shouted orders carried clearly to where they stood.

He reluctantly handed the flashlight over, and Peter and Kate headed toward the farm the back way. "Here, take this," Peter said, giving the light to Kate. He pulled out the throwaway phone. "I'm going to call Webb."

Kate did her best to keep up with Peter's long legs while attempting to shine the light so it hit the lumpy grass in front of them both. With every footfall, the refrain of "Vivi" and "Bebe" went through her mind. *What is going on at the farm?* She resolutely kept her thoughts from straying to horrific scenarios, focusing instead on getting there.

"He's not answering. Something must've happened to him." Peter grunted in disgust and dialed again. "Dispatch? Send units to Bluebonnet Farm." He gave the specific address. "All units are busy at Eagle Motor Sports? Yeah, I know that. I just came from there. Do what you can. ASAP." He shoved the phone into his pocket and grabbed Kate's arm. "Let's hustle."

From a map included in the article about the land dispute, Kate had a vague idea which direction the farm was in. Apparently Peter had also studied the lay of the land. He beelined through the fields right to the boundary stream. "Jump," he said when they reached it. Kate took a flying leap and landed on the other side, her boots squishing in the mud.

"To my truck first," Peter said, gasping for air as they dashed through a copse of trees. "My gun."

As they approached where he'd parked behind the retreat center, he signaled for her to turn off the flashlight. They stopped in the bushes and peered out at the buildings. No movement. The retreat center was dark, but lights shone on the first floor of the farmhouse from the kitchen and living room. Peter crept across the graveled parking area and opened his truck door with the key. Kate could see him fumbling around inside. Then, leaving the door open, he tiptoed back to join her.

"Need to find Webb," he whispered into her ear. They kept to the grass so their boots wouldn't crunch on the stones.

A police cruiser sat midway down the drive, headlights off and the driver's door open. As they drew closer, Kate's pulse leaped when she spotted a dark shape lying on the ground near the car. Peter gave a muffled groan and hurried over. By the light of the dashboard, she saw it was Deputy Webb, lying faceup, eyes closed. Peter stooped down and felt for his pulse. "He's alive." Standing up, he gazed around, searching for the assailant.

"They must be in the house," Kate whispered, her insides cold with fear. Unless the intruder had come and gone. Again, she thrust her thoughts away from imagining the worst.

Peter went farther down the drive, and she heard his muffled voice speaking to dispatch again. "Officer down" was all she heard clearly. She stared at the house, praying fiercely for the safety of her friends.

Peter came back up the drive, gesturing for her to join him as he moved silently toward the house. They worked their way through the garden, crouching low to stay out of the light spilling through the living room French doors. As she gently pushed aside the arching branches of a blossoming forsythia, she felt something pull on the back of her shirt.

The shock sent a rush of blood to her head, and her heart stopped. She opened her mouth to scream, but before she could get a sound out, she heard, "Kate, it's me." Vivi was hunkered down in the bushes. "I've been waiting for you to get here."

Relief that it was her friend and she was safe made Kate weak. She bent over, propping her hands on her knees, trying to breathe.

Peter noticed that Kate had stopped and returned. "Vivi! What happened?" he whispered.

"Derek and another man arrived at the house. I was in the kitchen, so I only saw them down the hall. They went into the living room. After I heard Bebe scream, I ran out the back door. I don't think they know I'm here."

Peter put up a hand for them to wait as he moved toward the partially open French door. Curious, Kate moved slightly closer so she could see inside.

Bebe and Derek were sitting in chairs, their hands and feet bound with duct tape. The tall cowboy she'd seen at Slim's convenience store—the one with big feet—paced back and forth in front of them, waving a gun. Unfortunately, Bebe and Derek were in the line of fire if shots were exchanged.

Peter rejoined them. "I think he's planning to stage a murder-suicide." He glanced at his watch. "I have no idea how long backup is going to take." He paused. "There's a big bust at Slim's," he added for Vivi's benefit.

Vivi's mouth twisted in fear and desperation as she hugged herself and swayed back and forth. "What should we do?"

Kate hated the idea of standing by helplessly while Bebe and Derek were in danger. The cowboy could decide to kill them at any moment. Her eyes skittered around the yard, wild ideas flashing into her mind. *What about a diversion?*

She noticed bales of straw mulch sitting in a stack near the garden fence. Then she remembered the candles and lanterns on the porch. "I have an idea. Let's start a fire to get that thug's attention."

Peter ran to the barn for an accelerant while Kate and

Vivi pulled the straw and some cut brush into a pile in the middle of a grassy area, far enough from the house to be safe. Peter doused the haystack with charcoal lighter fluid, then lit it with matches Kate had foraged from the porch.

Kate and Vivi ran out of sight to hide as the bone-dry straw flared into a plume of fire reaching about ten feet high, while Peter hid at the corner of the porch. Fortunately it was a still night, and sparks flew upward instead of blowing toward the house. The flames crackled and roared, reflecting off the house windows. As they hoped, it lured the cowboy out of the house.

"What the …?" He stood in the doorway, gun in hand, then stepped onto the porch and out into the yard. He stared at the mesmerizing flames dancing and leaping into the air.

Peter rushed forward, shovel in hand, and walloped the man on the back of the head. He collapsed into a heap on the ground, gun flying, his big feet bouncing once before lying still.

Twenty-One

While Peter cuffed the cowboy, Kate and Vivi dashed into the house to assist Bebe and Derek.

"Oh, thank goodness you're all right, Vivi!" Bebe said as Kate sawed at the duct tape on her wrists with a kitchen knife. "I was worried sick about you."

Vivi was helping Derek free himself. "I ran outside when I heard you scream. Then Peter and Kate showed up just in time."

"We got Vivi's text," Kate said. "Right before the police busted Slim's gambling joint, he told Peter the problem with you was 'being resolved tonight.' So we had more than one reason to hightail it out of there."

"I'm so sorry, Bebe," Derek said, his voice heavy with remorse. "I had no idea he was going to hurt you. I feel like a bloody fool for being involved with him in any way."

"That's because you are one," Bebe said tartly. "Why were you involved with a creep like Slim Baker anyway?" She rubbed angrily at the residue the tape had left on her wrists.

Derek lowered his eyes. "What can I say? My weaknesses got the better of me, my dear. "

Kate released the last of the tape from Bebe's ankles, and she sprang to her feet. "Thanks, Kate." She whirled on her ex-husband and shook her finger in his face. "Smarten up or you're going to lose Ariel. She's the best thing that ever happened to you." She paused. "Make that the second best."

"One thing I don't understand," said Kate, turning to

Derek. "How did your shoe tassel end up in the greenhouse? After the incident with the fan, I was sure you were involved in the attempts on Bebe's life."

"My shoe tassel?" Derek asked. "I didn't even know it was missing. It is rare, but I have been in the greenhouse. Or I suppose I could have lost it on the ground somewhere and Bebe's silly pet hen could have pecked at it and carried it in there."

He turned to Bebe.

"One thing I can assure you, my dear," he said. "I would never harm you."

Blue lights whirled in the yard. The cavalry had arrived.

The curtains parted and a handsome young man walked out onto the stage. "Ladies and gentlemen, welcome to 'That '70s Fashion Show.'" The crowd filling the Hamilton Arms Hotel ballroom burst into cheers as they recognized movie star Logan Lariby.

"I can't believe you got him as emcee," Vivi said to Kate. They, along with Paige, were watching from backstage where their job was to help Vanessa and her friends change. Peter and Patrick were helping the men. Derek was the event photographer, and the local television station was also filming.

"Vanessa has known him for years," Kate said. "And when she found out he was filming a Western in Dallas, she called him." Logan's addition to the lineup had meant they'd gotten tons of press coverage, and the 2,000-seat ballroom had sold out.

Bebe, resplendent in an icy blue couture gown, sashayed

onto the stage to join Logan. She took the microphone. "Hello, everyone. I'm Bebe." The audience cheered again in homage to the fashion icon. "Tonight we're going to experience a real blast from the past, a look at the rocking, retro, *ridiculous* fashions of the original 'Don't Decade,' the 1970s."

To the beat of a popular song from the era, the first group of models sauntered out. They wore Afro wigs and the widest bell-bottoms ever seen, along with peasant blouses, striped shirts, and platform shoes. Vanessa and the other models had choreographed synchronized steps, and the lines of men and women wove back and forth in formation to the music in an echo of the clothing's kooky vibe.

Paige clapped her hands. "It's utterly delightful."

Mary Benson bustled up, carrying a clipboard. "The velvet outfits are next, right?"

Vivi glanced at the sheet. "That's right. We'll be right in to help."

"I'm so glad everything got straightened out for her," Paige said as Mary scurried back to the dressing room.

"Me too," Kate said. It turned out the cowboy had hit Mary on the head during an argument at the farm. She hadn't wanted to continue being Slim Baker's spy since she really liked Bebe. She'd gone into hiding from Slim, a matter complicated by Vink's appearance.

Phoebe had doctored the tea in a misguided effort to redeem herself in Slim's eyes after messing up the assignment. She had also hoped to become the third Mrs. Baker despite their difference in age. She was in jail awaiting trial for attempted murder.

"I heard Mary got a job at the shelter," Vivi said. Paige nodded. "Yes, she's going to be assistant director."

The models pranced off the stage, and Kate hurried to help

them change. For the next set, the men wore crushed-velvet suits, long wigs, and lace-trimmed shirts. The women wore long velvet dresses and high-laced boots.

On it went, group after group of interesting and quirky outfits with commentary by Bebe and funny remarks from Logan. The last vignette included Kate's designs in the set "'70s Renaissance." After the rest of the models were onstage, Ariel emerged wearing the centerpiece of Kate's collection, a pink halter dress with a chevron pattern on the flowing skirt. Mist from dry ice on the stage added a touch of fantasy as the others fell back, allowing her to come forward. Even Kate gasped, a chill going down her spine as the dress she'd pictured in her mind came to life so beautifully. This project was shaping up to be the best work she'd accomplished so far.

"Isn't everything just stunning?" Bebe said. "The crochet in this tableau was all designed by our one and only Kate Stevens." The spotlight danced around, seeking Kate, who ducked further into the wings. Vivi and Paige grabbed her and pushed her out onto the stage. Feeling extremely foolish, she waved to the audience and joined Bebe, Ariel, and Logan. Now she was thankful that she had worn a beautiful, long, silvery crochet dress of her own design. She bowed to great applause and was grateful when Bebe next called on Paige and Vivi as organizers of the event.

"We raised enough tonight to support the Sparrow's Nest for a year," Bebe announced as she handed Paige a huge faux check representing the donation. The crowd roared, and the models emerged dressed in whichever outfit they had liked most. A disco song came on, and they began to dance in the background.

Peter, Patrick, and the other helpers came out onstage for a bow. Then Peter edged his way over to Kate. "Would you like to dance?" In honor of the occasion, he was dressed in denim bell-bottoms and a jean jacket. His belt buckle was a huge peace sign.

She shook her head, laughing. As he began to gyrate in front of her, she said, "Oh, why not?" On the floor, people were picking up chairs to make room, and most of the audience was also dancing. Derek was madly snapping shots, and the camera crew was panning the crowd, zooming in as some of the guests "busted a move" from the era.

Logan had put down his microphone and was now swinging Vanessa around in the intricate steps of the hustle. Some of the other dancers pulled back to watch, and naturally the video camera zeroed in on them.

"I bet you'll get clips on major news networks now," Peter said into Kate's ear. "Who knew Logan Lariby could dance like John Travolta?" Peter had his arm around Kate's waist, and they clasped hands.

"I hope we do. It'll help the shelter." In particular, the outpouring of generosity and support from Bebe, Logan, Derek, and Ariel awed her. "We've got some very special friends." That included Vivi, who was dancing nearby with Sam.

"Yes, we do." Peter let go of her waist to spin her in a circle. As she whirled back into his arms, he added, "And I've got a very special partner in you."

She gazed up into his deep blue eyes.

"I'm talking about it all, Kate. Work, dancing, and yes"—he kissed her warmly— "love."

Learn more about Annie's fiction books at

AnniesFiction.com

- Access your e-books
- Discover exciting new series
- Read sample chapters
- Watch video book trailers
- Share your feedback

We've designed the Annie's Fiction website especially for you!

Plus, manage your account online!

- Check your account status
- Make payments online
- Update your address

ANNIE'S ATTIC
MYSTERIES®

CREATIVE WOMAN
MYSTERIES®

Annie's Quilted Mysteries™

Annie's Mysteries Unraveled™

Visit us at AnniesFiction.com